I AM
MORGAN le FAY

A Tale from Camelot

NANCY SPRINGER

AN IMPRINT OF PENGUIN PUTNAM INC.

To Brian, Angie, and Travis,
with thanks for everyday heroism

FIREBIRD
Published by the Penguin Group
Penguin Putnam Inc., 345 Hudson Street, New York, New York 10014, U.S.A.
Penguin Books Ltd, 80 Strand, London WC2R ORL, England
Penguin Books Australia Ltd, Ringwood, Victoria, Australia
Penguin Books Canada Ltd, 10 Alcorn Avenue, Toronto, Ontario, Canada M4V 3B2
Penguin Books (N.Z.) Ltd, 182-190 Wairau Road, Auckland 10, New Zealand

Penguin Books Ltd, Registered Offices: Harmondsworth, Middlesex, England

First published in the United States of America by Philomel Books,
a division of Penguin Putnam Books for Young Readers, 2001
Published by Firebird, an imprint of Penguin Putnam Inc., 2002

1 3 5 7 9 10 8 6 4 2

THE LIBRARY OF CONGRESS HAS CATALOGED THE PHILOMEL EDITION AS FOLLOWS:
Springer, Nancy.
I am Morgan le Fay : a tale from Camelot / Nancy Springer.
p. cm.
Summary: In a war-torn England where her half brother Arthur will eventually
become king, the young Morgan le Fay comes to realize that
she has magic powers and links to the faerie world.
1. Morgan le Fay (Legendary character)—Juvenile fiction. [1. Morgan le Fay
(Legendary character)—Fiction. 2. Magic—Fiction. 3. Fairies—Fiction.
4. Knights and knighthood—Fiction. 5. England—Fiction.
6. Arthur, King—Fiction.] I. Title.
PZ7.S76846 Iaap 2001 [Fic]—dc21
99-052847
ISBN 0-399-23451-9 (hc)

ISBN 0-698-11974-6

Printed in the United States of America

Prologue

SEATED AT THE HIGH TABLE, WITH THE EMERALD NECK-lace her husband had given her resting on her half-naked bosom, the emerald tiara nestled in her dark hair, Lady Igraine tried not to answer the leer of the king. After years of warring with the duke—her husband—why now had the king suddenly called a truce and summoned them to his court? Why was he now feasting them? And why was he ogling her so?

She tried to listen to the minstrels playing upon lute and viol—music was a rare treat, but it could not cheer her. Nor did the sweet fragrance of scented beeswax raise her spirits, or the way candlelight glowed upon vessels of pure tooled gold. Al-though the servants placed before her roast suckling pig, quail in pomegranate sauce, sweetmeats, plum pudding, and many other delicacies, Igraine ate little. At last the marzipan was served and it was over. She rose to rejoin her husband, who was seated near the king, next to that fearsome old sorcerer who served as the king's chief counselor. A look into the dark pits of the sorcerer's eyes made Igraine shudder almost as much as her spidery sense of the king's stare on her bare shoulders.

Lifting her heavy silk skirt a few inches to free her slippered feet, Igraine took a couple of steps toward her husband. But the king stood in her way.

"Lady Igraine," he said, grasping her hand and pressing it to his lips.

She curtsied without replying. Perhaps she blushed, although she hated herself for blushing—but he was kissing her hand more than once, far more than courtesy called for. She wanted to pull her hand away, but did not dare. He was the king.

"Igraine the Beautiful," he told her in a low, vibrant voice, "there will be peace if only you will be my paramour."

Panic stabbed her; her heart pounded. With a word she could save the lives of many, many men—but her husband! How could she betray her husband? Did this lecherous king not know what it meant for a woman to love and be loyal to her husband?

"What say you, my lovely Igraine?"

"I say no, Your Majesty." Her voice trembled. She wished it would not tremble, but it did. So did her hand.

The king scowled. "What?"

"By your leave," she quavered, pulling her hand away from him. She fled to her husband's side.

"What is the matter?" he asked her.

"Shhh."

Later, in their bedchamber, she told him. He leaped up and started slinging on his armor. "I'll kill him!"

"No, darling, think what—"

"He must die. I'll kill him now. As he sleeps."

"Dear heart, there are guards! You'll be one against many! You'll be slain."

"I care not. I will kill him."

"And if he kills you instead, what will become of me?"

He faced her without speaking.

"Let us take to horse," Igraine said, "and leave this place at once."

They did so, making their escape in the night. When the king heard of their flight, he was enraged. He sent a messenger after them with word that they could expect either to be dead or be his prisoners within six weeks.

The duke manned and provisioned his two strongest castles, one for his wife and one for himself. Although Igraine understood that they separated for her safety—for the king would attack the duke first—still, she missed her husband dreadfully. Four, five, six weeks the king and his army besieged the duke's castle. Igraine paced the battlements every day. Even the playful hugs of her little daughters, Morgause and Morgan, could not comfort her.

Daughters. Two daughters, and her husband loved her still, even though she had not given him a son. Her heart swelled with longing for him.

On a night of the dark of the moon, she lay abed in her lonely chamber—although not yet sleeping—when she heard the surprised cries of servants in the hallway. Her chamber door opened and her husband strode in.

"Darling!" She sprang up to meet him. He looked weary and grimy from weeks in the field.

Without a word he took her into his arms.

She gave herself to him utterly. But something was wrong. He did not speak to her; he did not whisper endearments to her. He did not caress her as he usually did. It was as if she had given herself to a stranger.

At dawn he arose, kissed her silently and left her.

She gazed after him, longing for something more, some sign. And perhaps it was a sign she saw, but a freakish one. As he passed through the chamber door, beyond it she saw the wolfish gleam of eyes, one glimmering green, the other eerily purple. Igraine knew those fey mismatched eyes: her younger daughter, Morgan, roaming the shadows like a restless spirit.

Then the door closed.

Igraine lay for a while staring into the shadows of the ceiling groins, then called for her women to help her dress. She refused breakfast. An uncanny knowledge rode in her belly: She carried a son from the night just past.

She climbed the spiral stairs of her tower. At the top, standing upon the windy battlements, she looked up—and shuddered. Over her head hovered a great soot gray carrion bird. It answered her stare with its pale, beady eye, then gave a harsh cry and flapped away.

Dread clawed Igraine's heart as she descended to the great hall.

Messengers awaited her. Her husband was dead, they told her. After seeing the king ride away from his encampment, the duke had sallied forth in a nighttime attempt to lift the siege. He had been killed.

He had been killed some four hours before dawn. Four hours before he had kissed her good-bye.

BOOK ONE
Caer Tintagel

1

My FATHER LOVED ME.

He was the only one ever to love me truly.

They killed him when I was six years old.

I am Morgan le Fay, and I will never die. I hover on the wind, and fate falls out of each slow beat of my wings. That is what my name means: Morgan the fate, Morgan the magical, fey Morgan of the otherworld, Morgan who must be feared. But I was not always Morgan le Fay. When they killed my father, I was only little Morgan.

I saw him once after he was dead. I will never forget that night.

While he yet lived, I saw him perhaps eight or ten times that I remember. My father was the Duke of Cornwall, and he was often absent, at war. At first I thought he went out to fight a dragon. Later I understood that he fought a king with an odd name, something about a penned dragon. I did not understand or care what the battles were about; it was the nature of

3

noblemen, evidently, to fight one another, and my father was very much a lord and a warrior.

When he came home to Tintagel, the whole castle shouted and sprang up to make him welcome. Nurse would restrain me with one hand and my sister, Morgause, with the other, for we were lady born, not common urchins to go capering under the horses' feet. We had to stand on the steps of the keep and watch with dignity, like Mother, as Father rode in at the gate, his head lifted so that his russet beard jutted from under his helm, his mail jingling and shining, his war horse curveting under his spurs. When he dismounted, he would look first to my mother, Igraine the Beautiful—that was what folk called her, and they did not lie. She was like moonlight on the sea, a goddess made of starlight and shadows. Proudly she would descend to meet him, my father, and he would look only at her, he would not even glance at me, and I would feel a fire dragon burning in my heart even though all the servants would cheer crazily. Father would toss his reins to a page boy and give Mother his hand. Hand in hand they would walk to the tall arched doorway and go inside.

Then no one would see them for a while. Father and Mother would go somewhere by themselves. And the castle folk would cheer and laugh and talk and joke. But Nurse never let Morgause and me hear the talk, the joking. She would take us back to our tower chamber, where she would scrub us. She would wash our hair and brush it and plait it with cord of gold and wind it around our heads so that it looked like a crown made of braids. She would put us in our best frocks, with hose and shoes.

Then we would wait.

Nurse would try to feed us porridge and milk for supper but we could not eat.

And then. Then, finally, my father would send for us.

In his chamber amid torchlight and shadows he was a warm glow awaiting us in the big red velvet chair. Now he was not a mailed warrior; now he wore a soft woolen tunic and smelled of tallow soap. He would open his arms to us and hug us each to one side of his chest and kiss us amid his prickly beard and perch us each on one burly knee and turn his smile and his shining gray eyes upon each of us. "So, Morgan." He would address me first, for I was his favorite. "My little firebrand, how goes the mischief these days?"

And I could tell him anything fearlessly. "I put the cat in the wash water, Daddy!"

"I *heard*. Kitty came out very clean and the linens very dirty."

"And I ran away from Nurse. I ran outside in my small-clothes."

"So I am told!"

"And I climbed the big pear tree and tore my apron."

And my father would say proudly, "You are born for trouble, Morgan."

That was why I loved my father so, because he saw me truly. He looked in my eyes and he knew. Morgause and I had dark eyes, deer eyes like our mother's, but mine were not quite like: One of my eyes peeped shadowy emerald green, and one violet, like deepest dusky amethyst. My eyes marked me as fey right from the start. Most folk did not notice—they just saw dark eyes, almost black—or they chose not to notice. To all the others, even my mother, my sister and I were a sort of two-

5

headed animal called Morgan-Morgause or, more commonly, "Girls!" Although Morgause was a year older, we might as well have been twins. They dressed us alike, lessoned us alike, scolded us alike when our noses were dirty and exhorted us alike to sit still and keep our legs together. But Daddy and I knew that I was not the least bit like prissy Morgause.

"And how is my beautiful Morgause?" he would ask her next. He never called me beautiful, even though Morgause and I looked much alike, with our mother's porcelain skin and smooth sable hair. I knew we looked alike because folk said so, and also because Mother sometimes let us look at ourselves in her mirror. Father had gifted her with it, a mirror of polished silver, worthy of a queen. Most noblewomen had a circle of polished bronze for a mirror if they had any at all.

I did not mind that Daddy did not call me beautiful, because it took nothing to be beautiful, and I knew he liked my mischief better.

"I've been good, Daddy," Morgause would answer, almost in a whisper.

"I knew it." He would give us each a hug. "You're my good little girl. And Morgan here is my most excellent daredevil. You're like scabbard and sword. You go together."

Then he would hug each of us again and kiss us again and send us off to bed with a gentle swat to hurry us on our way.

The swat did no good in my case. I was not one to stay in bed.

Morgause and I slept in the same chamber, with Nurse on a pallet between us. Nurse snored. Morgause slept quiet as a mouse all night long, flat on her back with her hands outside the coverlet the way Nurse told us to lie. I slept sometimes.

More often I lay awake and wondered about things: What was war for? Was it fun? Why did women not do it? Why did women always have to keep their legs together, even on horses, riding sideways? Why must I keep my hands outside the coverlet?

And sometimes, quite often actually, I grew weary of lying on my back with my hands to my chin and I grew weary of wondering and I got up out of bed, crept past Nurse and out of the chamber, and wandered the shadowy corridors of the castle. Often I drifted toward my mother's chamber, for my mother was a great mystery to me. Once a day I was brought to her to be inspected and chided and kissed, but other than that I seldom saw her. And other than on those occasions I never entered my mother's chamber. I would wander there only in the night sometimes, and stand cold and barefoot staring at her closed door awhile, and wander away again.

So it was that I saw my father one last time, after he was dead.

It was a night of the dark of the moon, very silent. I heard no owl call. Even the dogs down in the village beyond the wall were silent, and even the sea washed quietly against the rocky cliffs below the castle walls on that night, and the wind for once was still. I ghosted through the great hall, gazing up into the vast vaulting shadows of the groins, and I wished I could slip out to the kennels or the mews, but the guards might see me there. So I drifted up to the darkened solarium instead— through the costly glass windows I could see just a whisper of light in the east. Dawn. I must return to my bed soon so that Nurse would find me there in the morning, or else she would scold. Not that I much minded her scolding. Nurse was a plain, blocky Cornishwoman, perhaps of middle age; she seemed to me as old as the mountains, and as blank and patient. She never beat me. Nor did she ever speak a word more than was necessary. I understood that, being a sandy-haired commoner, she was different from my sleek, dark-haired, finely bred Breton mother, different from my sister and me.

After all, I did not much care about getting back to my bed before dawn. I wandered toward my mother's chamber.

And as I padded toward her door, it opened and my father, fully armed, strode out.

I was so surprised that I could not even shout. "Daddy!" I squeaked, and I ran toward him with my arms flung wide.

He barely looked at me. He shoved me out of the way with one gloved hand, sending me sprawling, and strode on.

I could not comprehend. I could only react. "Daddy!" I whimpered, and I picked myself up and trotted after him.

I could not catch up with him. His stride was longer than two of mine, even when I ran. But I followed him down the corridor and the spiral stairs and another long corridor to a postern gate where guards with torches and men on horses awaited him.

"Did it go as planned, Sire?"

I froze in my steps, for I could not find courage to move another inch toward the man who had spoken. His eyes—were those eyes? I saw them as black pits amid his steel gray beard. He wore a black gown bordered in stars and moons and strange devices that shone with their own weird green glow in the half-light. Instead of riding a horse, he rode a long-eared white mule. Although I stood in the shadows, he looked straight at me and smiled—it was as if a skull had grinned at me. And a fey and fearsome shock of recognition burned through me, even though I had never seen such a person before.

Sorcerer.

"Just as planned," said my father—but his voice was not my father's voice. Daddy's voice was slow and golden, like honey, but this strange daddy's voice was like the scratch of dog claws on gravel. Swinging onto his horse, a fat, brass-colored charger I had never seen before, he said, "I owe you a purse of gold, Merlin."

"No, Sire. You owe me only what you have promised."

A look passed between them. I cowered; I could not have withstood looking into that wizard's empty black gaze.

"The baby she will bear," said the Sire man in a low voice. "Do not forget, my king, or you will rue it."

"I keep my promises. But what do you want with my son?"

Merlin only laughed. He laughed like a night bird as they rode away.

I slipped back to my bed and lay trembling with my hands naughtily under the covers, curled between my legs for warmth. After a while I slept.

Oddly, Nurse let us girls sleep late that morning. When we awoke, we saw that she had been crying. She gave us porridge to eat, then told us that our father was dead.

I did not understand *dead*. I understood only that Daddy was gone. Somehow he had been turned into this Sire person, who turned out to be Uther Pendragon.

I did not think to fear that I would lose my mother also.

Nurse put us in our plainest frocks—brown wool—with

brown hose and shoes. She brushed our hair smooth but let it hang loose down our backs. All the while Morgause cried, squeakily, like the mouse she was, until she hiccuped. But I did not weep. I turned to stone.

When she had dressed us, Nurse took us to our mother and left us.

Perhaps she thought that our mother would comfort us, or that we would comfort her. But no. Mother sat dressed only in a chemise—I had never seen her so, and she seemed to me even more beautiful that way, in that simple shift of white, than when she wore silks and velvets and jewels. Her dark hair flowed loose like mine, rippling down over her pale, naked shoulders. She sat at her chamber window and stared. Morgause ran to her and laid her head in her lap, weeping, but Mother did not move. She did not even lower her eyes from their staring. She sat like a lovely statue and let Morgause weep upon her.

There were servants in the room, but they either wept upon one another or stood behind Mother, staring eastward as she did. I studied Mother for a while. Then, as she did not move— no one moved—I turned to the door, lugged it open with my heels digging deep into the scented rushes on the floor, and went out.

No one seemed interested in keeping me from wandering. I looked over my shoulder for a moment at the door that had closed behind me, then pattered off to see what was happening elsewhere.

In the kitchen they were cooking clothes. I had never seen such a thing. A huge pot boiling, and clothes going into it and coming out drippy black, like wet crows. I saw my favorite frock, red with blue larkspur trim, go in, and I cried out and ran forward to try to save it. I would have dived into the vat after it, and been boiled black in my turn, but one of the cooks seized me. Without scolding, without even speaking, she put me out the door.

I wept for the frock as I had not wept for my father, and I ran out into the courtyard, its cobbles ever shadowed by high walls. Beyond those walls the sea crashed cold against the cliffs, and always the wind swept down raw off the moors, but although I wore no shawl, I did not feel the chill. I was a weeping stone; what did I care whether the wind blew?

Where was everyone?

The gates stood open. No guards. No one coming or going atop the walls or within them.

I stopped weeping but kept running. I ran out through the yawning gates, past the village huts huddled against the outside of the wall, and up the rugged grazing lands toward the moor.

In that high place there were no people, only furze and heather and stunted thorn trees, deer and foxes and wind and stones. But giants used to live on the moor, Nurse had told me. Great stones taller than two men stood on end where the giants had placed them, maybe to play at quoits, for huge hoop-shaped stones lay strewn here and there. They must have been playful giants, because they had balanced the logan stones atop the cliffs also, stones the size of six horses, yet they rocked in every breeze as gently as cradles. The giants were gone now, Nurse said. Heroes had thrown them into the sea. Once I had asked her if Daddy had ever thrown a giant into the sea and she had laughed, but then she had said yes, he might have done so.

Maybe Daddy was in the sea now. Maybe a giant had come back and thrown him in. Maybe that was why everyone was acting so strange.

The steep moor slowed me to a walk. I trudged up the rocky hillside with no idea where I was going or why. In the distance, dust rose. That meant horsemen coming. Usually it meant Daddy coming home, and the castle folk would shout and Mother would come out and stand on the steps of the keep.

I did not know what it meant this time.

Caer Tintagel looked small below me now. Silent. Gates open like a beached fish's mouth.

I came to a circle stone standing on edge, bigger than a millstone, with a hole through it larger than I was tall. I climbed into the hole, turned sideways to make myself part of the stone and sat, waiting.

The dust had come closer, and in it I could see ghostlike shapes of men walking, silent, their heads down, their hands behind them. The ones on horses, the knights, herded the walking men like cattle, prodding them with their spears.

After that came more knights riding double file with their lances raised and in the fore a flag flying. A giant flag shaped like flames. Then I saw that the flames had form. A red dragon.

The wind made the dragon seem alive. I slipped through the quoit stone and lay on the ground behind it, hiding. I saw no more.

Perhaps that is what made such a difference between me and Morgause, afterward: that she saw Uther Pendragon ride into Tintagel, driving his prisoners before him, and she saw Mother walk out, barefoot and proud and pale in only her chemise, to surrender our home to him. And that I did not.

It was not until years afterward that I understood how Uther Pendragon had tricked Mother with Merlin's magic illusion the night before and bedded her. She never spoke of it.

I lay behind the quoit stone—some folk said such stones had a magical power to heal a person who passed through them, but it had done nothing for me. I lay there and after a while I realized I was shaking all over, maybe with cold, and digging my fingers deep into the slaty ground. I sat up and saw that my hands were dirty and bloody red from clawing at the shale.

One hand clutched something, I noticed as if the hand did not belong to me. I willed it to open, and it did. In the palm lay a small something so round it could not have been just a pebble. I stood up and dropped it into the pocket of my brown frock.

Over the sea the sun was setting as red as my blood. As red as the dragon flag. In the waves its reflection shifted like flames.

I knew I had to go home.

Yet I did not see how I could bear to.

Something sniffed at my ankle. I looked down, so stony numb I was not even surprised. A black dog stood there, neither friendly nor fierce, gazing at me with weird white eyes.

"Child," said a voice behind me.

I turned, and at first I thought it was a giant looming over me. But it was Merlin, hard and dark like a standing stone in the dusk. He wore a coarse cloak, like a shepherd's mantle, and he carried a thick, knotty walking stick, but I knew him. I could never mistake that voice like winter thistles or those black pits, like tin mines, that were his eyes. It was he.

I had no strength left to scream. I just stared into the midnight of his eyes, and he stared into the green and purple twilight of mine.

"Fay," he whispered.

I had not yet heard it then, for no one except my father considered me of much account, but my mismatched eyes marked me as one set apart. Morgan le Fay.

"Fate upon fate," Merlin murmured. "Cycles upon cycles of fate. Who are you, child?"

I could not speak. I tried to back away, but my feet seemed not to work.

"There is the ancient green power here," he said. "I smell it. What is your name, child? Is it Morrigun?"

At last my panic gave me strength. I ran. Headlong, falling down the slope, cutting my knees on the rocks, I ran back to Tintagel and reached it just as the gates were closing.

The courtyard teemed with strangers. Nobody seemed to notice a bloody child running through. I reached my chamber and found Morgause there, and she looked at me as if I were a stranger, her face as pallid and flat as the moon. Nurse came in after a while, took me to the washstand and scrubbed me and bandaged my hands and knees, all in silence. She did not scold me or ask me where I had been. I concluded that no one had missed me. Since Daddy was gone, no one cared.

2

THREE DAYS LATER, UTHER PENDRAGON TOOK MY mother away.

Nurse led me and Morgause to the steps of the keep and stood there holding us by the hands, just as if we were watching Daddy ride off to war. I stared at the huge warhorse. It was the same fat, brass-colored horse Daddy had mounted in the dawn, but on that horse now sat Uther Pendragon, and he was not like Daddy at all. He did not look at us. In the three days he had spent in Tintagel, taking charge and appointing his own steward to run the castle, he had not once looked at us or spoken to us. His charger pawed at the cobbles a few feet from us, but Uther Pendragon stared eastward, where his stronghold, Caer Argent, awaited him. His eyes glinted sharp and dark, like flints.

"Stand!" he ordered his horse, curbing it sharply. His voice was the scratchy, dog-claws-on-gravel voice of the daddy I had seen in the night.

Small wonder I barely understood anything that was happening.

Mother came out with her maids-in-waiting clustered in a half circle around her as if to protect her. But the maids drew back as Mother crouched before my sister and me and hugged us one by one. She did not speak. Nor did she weep. She kissed us—her face felt cold, like a smooth white stone, against mine. Morgause and I wore our black-dyed frocks, but Mother wore a green silk gown with an overgown of gold; later I learned that her new lord and master would not allow her the black mourning dress of a widow.

There was much that I did not learn until years later. I did not think to wonder at the time where my father's body was, or why there had been no funeral. I did not know that his head had been paraded on a pike and the crows had picked out his kind gray eyes. I did not know that his body had been looted, then left on the battlefield, food for the carrion birds as well. And because I had not seen his dead body, I did not understand. Dead? I had seen dead leaves, but leaves sprang green again in the spring. I had seen dead trees send up shoots that grew into saplings. I had seen a cook make a chicken dead for the pot, but surely no one had wrung my father's strong neck.

If Mother was going away with this strange, flinty king, it had to be because he was Daddy now. No other explanation made sense.

Except—maybe it was all my fault. Because I was bad, because I had so much trouble in me, Daddy was gone and Mother was leaving.

She hugged Morgause one more time, then without a word she stepped into the canopied horse litter and settled herself on the cushions. Someone was crying, but it was not me. It was one of Mother's women weeping as she wrapped a fur mantle around Mother's narrow shoulders.

Then they drew the curtains around Mother, and I saw her no more. Uther Pendragon barked out something, and many horses started to walk at once, horses of knights and men-at-arms and the litter horses carrying Mother away. I remember the sound of many hooves clopping hollow on the cobbles, making me think of raindrops, although for once in that wet land no rain was falling; only a morning mist hung in the air. After the gates closed behind them there was nothing to hear but the roar of the sea pounding, beating, raging against the rocks below Tintagel.

"Come," Nurse said, leading us by the hands into the keep again.

"Is Mother going to war now?" I asked, trotting to keep up. For a six-year-old I was small.

"No."

Morgause started crying. The goose, why was she crying? Mother had hugged her last. Mother had hugged her more than me.

I demanded of Nurse, "Is Mother going to be with Daddy?"

"No."

"Where is she going, then?"

"To be married."

But Mother was married to Daddy. "Will she come back soon?"

"No."

Nothing made sense.

◆ ◆ ◆

17

It might have been that day, or the next, or the next week, that Nurse picked up my brown frock to go cook it black like the others and something fell out of the pocket and rolled into the rushes on the chamber floor.

"What was that?" she asked.

I said, "Nothing."

"How so, nothing?"

"Nothing but a pebble I found."

Nurse went away. Morgause kept on playing with her doll. "Now put on your black dress," she told it. The doll did not have a black dress; it was made of unbleached wool and its dress was the same color. I had torn the head off my doll and I wanted to tear the heads off Morgause's doll and Morgause as well. Instead, I hunted in the rushes and found the round something I had clawed out of the dirt below the quoit stone and forgotten ever since. I stood on the stool before the wash-basin and plunked my find into the water.

Then I gawked and gasped.

A pebble should sink. This did not. Nor did it float. Softly and quite unnaturally it swam like a tadpole or a minnow in the midst of the water, and the water eddied and roiled around it.

A dirty stone should need to be scrubbed. This did not. Like skirts swirling out from a dancing maiden, layers of brown drifted up, opening like veils cast off, revealing the glimmering azure wonder beneath.

I did not understand what it was, but I sensed that it had been under that quoit stone for a long, long time, maybe since the time of the giants, and that all that long time it had meant to find me.

It was small, no larger than the nail on my littlest finger, but so clear and shining blue that it seemed larger. Rain-washed sky, robin's egg, sunlit holy well—none were so blue as this. An angel's eyes might be so blue—and like an eye, this round thing had fine veins and a dark circle at its core. But the wormwork of veins glinted richly gold, not red, and the dark circle was not a pupil, but a hole.

I dared not stare too long—Nurse might come back. I glanced around to see whether Morgause had noticed my gasp—blessed be, she had not. "Now say bye-bye to Mommy," she cooed at her doll, laying it in the chest and closing the lid on it as if she were placing it in a coffin. I snatched my—stone, all I could think to call it was stone—I snatched it out of the water, hopped down from the stool and heaved open the chamber door, running out.

Even though it was wet, the stone felt warm in my hand.

I ran to my mother's chamber. If it could any longer be called my mother's chamber.

No one prevented me from pushing my way in, for there was no one there. The rushes had been swept out and the oak floor left bare. This was a high, sunny tower chamber, vaulted, with its great beams carved all over in forms of hounds and deer running and twisting together like puzzles and biting one another. It was a chamber fitting for the lady of the castle, too grand for any lesser person, and so it brooded on ghosts, empty.

My mother's chair, all gilt curves and velvet padding, still crouched at the window. Her embroidery basket still squatted beside it on the cold floor.

In that hollow, haunted place, under the carved wooden

gaze of many wild beasts, I opened my hand and looked at the stone. Warm like a baby sun in my palm, it shone with its own blue-gold watery light.

After looking at it for a while I somehow knew what to do.

I pattered over to my mother's chair, sat there, and rooted with my grubby little paws among the fine white linens in her basket. Among the cloth I found a thick silk thread, red as blood. It took my chubby fingers a while to string it through the hole in the stone, but I succeeded. It took even longer to knot the thread behind my neck, but I managed to do that also. Then I hid thread and stone under my frock. The stone lay as warm as a living thing upon my ribby, narrow chest, against my skin, over my heart.

I sat in my mother's chair, looked out her window to the east and wondered where she was.

That might have been her wedding day. It was a ten-day journey to Caer Argent. The moment he had conveyed her there, thirteen days after he had widowed her, Uther Pendragon wedded her, then bedded her.

A year passed. Morgause and I were allowed plain brown and white frocks now, and the black ones were put away. I turned seven years old, and Nurse tried to start me on sewing and embroidery. I hated it.

Out on the moor one day, curled in my quoit stone to hide from Nurse and the everlasting needlework, I paid no particular heed when a messenger rode into the castle. Messengers were always coming and going between Uther Pendragon and Redburke, his steward at Tintagel, a man I found remarkable chiefly for his bearish bad humor and his turnip nose. Twice a messenger reporting to Redburke had also brought small tokens from Mother for Morgause and me—once rings made of her hair, which we were not allowed to wear lest we spoil them, and once tiny red satin pincushions shaped like hearts. I did not like to stick pins in mine; it felt as if I were stabbing Mother. Messengers came often and such gifts seldom, so I expected nothing as I saw this particular lad on a fleet pony gallop in.

Great was my astonishment, then, when a few moments later he cantered out of the gates again, veered off the wagon track, and sent his pony surging straight up the moor to the quoit stone where I was hiding.

"Go in at once," he told me.

He was slim and young, maybe twelve years old, and he had addressed me rudely, without a greeting or a bow, as if I were a commoner like him. Still, I saw that he was very handsome, with curly black hair and a comely face and eyes almost as blue as my secret stone—for some reason as I looked up at him I felt aware of the secret stone nestled warm on my chest— and I admired the way he rode his dapple-gray pony, but he had ordered me to go in like a child and he was not *that* much older and I had not thought anyone knew of my hiding place, and altogether a moil of strong feelings converged in me and turned my astonishment to vexation.

"No," I said.

"You're Morgan, aren't you?" he said, patting his pony's neck as he spoke. The pony was as handsome as he, but in a pretty, yielding way, with its delicate head bowed and its dark eyes downcast and its forelock lying damp with sweat between them. Part of its mane had fallen over on the wrong side of its lovely arched neck. The messenger boy smoothed it back into place as he told me, "They want you to go in right away."

I did not move. "Why?"

Most likely he did not know and could not have answered me if he wanted to. Uther Pendragon was a lettered man, not a common king who might entrust his message to a boy, and he made sure that his stewards were lettered also. Only kings and lords and such were allowed to learn to read and write, not women and commoners, and the thought caused the fire dragon to rouse in my chest, for whatever kings and lords had I wanted also. I did not like having things kept from me, and I did not like being ordered around by this curly-haired boy who did not reply to my question.

Nor did his face show me any answer; he just swung down off his pony. He was used to dealing with balky creatures such as ponies and children, I suppose, and they did not bother him. He did not frown.

"Come on," he said.

"No!"

He wasted no time arguing, but picked me up out of the quoit stone with his two hands under my arms. I yelled like a cottage brat and kicked and struggled, but my thrashings did not trouble him. He placed me on the pony, astride in the saddle just as if I were a boy like he, slipped the reins forward over its sharp gray ears, and led off toward the castle gates.

I sat still and silent in surprise, fear, delight—mostly delight. I had never ridden a horse; no lady ever sat a horse, not even sideward, if she could help it. It had never occurred to me to ask to ride a horse, but I liked sitting high above the ground and feeling the pony swing along under me. I liked the smell of the sweaty animal and the sense of his power carrying me along. I liked the coarse strength of his grizzled mane in my clutching hands. I liked his twitching, black-tipped, fox-pricked ears.

Halfway down the moor I sat silent, and then I demanded, "What's his name?"

"The little horse? He's a she. She's Annie." The boy said this as fondly as if he spoke of a sister.

I burst out, "Give me the reins. I want to ride by myself."

Striding along at Annie's head, he glanced over his shoulder at me and shook his head. But he smiled—there was something very nice about his smile, not as if he were being kind but rather as if we had something in common, he and I. As if he had put me on the pony because he thought I might like it, and he was pleased that I did.

I asked, "What is your name?"

"Thomas."

I wanted to ask him more questions—how old Annie was, and how old he was, and how had it come about that he and Annie ran errands for the king. But I did not get to ask him anything more, for as we approached the gates Nurse came running out and seized me, swinging me down off Annie herself. I had not known she was so strong. I did not even have a chance to pat Annie good-bye as Nurse hurried me away.

"We're sent for," she said, hustling me up the steps of the keep at a trot.

I did not understand what *sent for* meant. But it was obvious that there had been some great event. "Is Daddy back?"

"No. Hush."

She did not speak again until we reached our chamber. The door hung open, and maidservants came and went with pitchers of hot water from the kitchen, filling a wooden tub. I was to be bathed? What had happened?

"Is Mother back?"

Nurse took a deep breath and uttered the longest sentence I had ever heard from her. "We're sent for to Caer Avalon to attend your lady mother and your new baby brother." She knelt and began to strip clothing off me.

New baby brother? For the second time that day astonishment gripped me. I did not think—

Nurse's swift hands faltered to a halt. I blinked, looked at her, and saw her staring at my bare chest.

Oh. Oh, no. Until then I had been able to hide my secret stone from her, slipping it under the mattress when my clothing was to be changed. But she had caught me by surprise, and there I stood with the stone glowing bluer than a cornflower on my skinny chest.

I smacked my hand over it, both hands, as if it were my privates and a man had caught me with my drawers down. "Mine!" I cried, terrified. Please, she must not take it away.

She lifted her gaze to my face, her eyes as wide as if she were an ox. She whispered, "Where did you get that?"

"It came to me! It's mine!"

She fixed me with her round, flat gaze for a good while. I do not know what she saw or what she thought—for she never mentioned my fey mismatched eyes, then or ever—but she nodded. "Yes," she murmured, "it is yours."

Something gentle and final in her voice gave me to know that it was so. My hands relaxed their grip on the stone, slip-

ping down so that she could see it again. I whispered to her, "What is it?"

"A milpreve."

It was not a word I had ever heard before. "What?"

"Druid stone."

I knew nothing of druids except that they were gone, like the giants. "It's old?"

"Yes."

So my mind had told me truth. I had known from the start that the stone was old.

Nurse said, "Powerful folk wore them long ago." I could see that she was struggling to explain. "Kings of the otherworld. And goddesses."

Otherworld? Goddesses?

"Eggs of the world serpent, some folk call them." Nurse shifted her gaze away from mine and set again about the task of taking off my clothes.

I was newly amazed. "A *snake* made it?"

Nurse gave me a long look such as I had never seen from her before. "I do not know," she said finally. "No one knows. Such stones go to those who are destined for them. Wear it with blessing and goodness in your heart, little Morgan."

She had never spoken to me so seriously or so tenderly before.

3

ALL THE WAY INLAND TO CAER AVALON, I SAT IN A trundling wagon and wished that I could ride a dapple-gray pony instead and outstrip the men-at-arms on their tall bay horses. All the way over the moors and down to the plain, Nurse sewed feverishly, trying to prepare finery for Morgause and me to wear to our baby brother's name-day. All the way, my druid stone rode secret against my chest, while a stone of some emotion I could not name rode hard and sharp in my heart, and Morgause and I quarreled for no reason.

"We're going to see Mo-ther," Morgause sang. "Going to see Mo-ther!"

Anyone with sense should know better than to sing out loud like that, tempting fate. I pinched her leg to make her stop.

"Ow!" She kicked me in the shin. "Stop it!" Then, of course, she sang again, "We're going to see—"

"*You* stop it!" I yelled.

"Why? I'm happy. We're going to see—"

I grabbed her by the braids and pulled her head down. She got out only a squeak before I clamped my hand over her mouth. Nurse was doing her best to ignore both of us. Knowing better, but hoping in a way, I sang, "We're going to see Dad-dy, going to see Dad-dy!"

Morgause struggled free from my grip and gasped, "Hush!"

I sang more loudly, "We're going to see Dad-dy—"

"We are not!"

"Yes, we are! Going to see—"

She smacked me and then started to sob as if I had hit her, not the other way around. "I hate you!" she yelled at me. "Stupid, Daddy's dead!"

"Stupid yourself! If there's a baby, there has to be a daddy!"

"Not *our* daddy!"

"Why not?" My face stung where she had hit me. I stuffed my hands under my skirted legs to keep from rubbing it; I did not want to give her that satisfaction.

Morgause wept harder. "U-U-Uth—that king what's-his-name is the daddy."

"But he *is* Daddy."

"You're crazy!"

I had not seen Mother walk out barefoot to surrender to Uther Pendragon. But Morgause had not seen Daddy walk out of Mother's bedchamber three hours after he was killed. Small wonder we seldom understood each other.

The wagon jounced on, and despite the canopy and curtains we choked in the dust kicked up by the men-at-arms in the fore, and I sometimes stopped tormenting Morgause long enough to gawk through the curtains at lands such as I had never seen. No sea cliffs and stony moors here. Instead, a vast grassy flatness swept level as a table to meet the sky, and even the sky seemed different, clear blue like my secret stone instead of rainbow misty, and from the surface of the flatness shone glimmers and meanders of blue like the blue of the sky, winding along the surface like the snaky gold veins of the milpreve. It took me a while to realize that I was seeing water—I knew the ocean waves thundering against the cliffs when I saw them, and the torrents dashing down over stones from the moors, but I had never seen such tame, flat blue water. Only when I saw ducks and wading birds in it did I recognize it. Then I felt foolish, and left off looking to tease Morgause again.

Nighttimes we slept on the ground, and it was a miserable business, especially when it rained. Traveling in general is a miserable business, especially bumping along in a wretched wagon, and I soon wearied of it, and of annoying my nurse and distressing my sister, and even of gawking at the strange lands through which we were toiling. A rift of jagged lavender between plain and sky occupied my attention for a while, but Nurse said it was distant tors, mountains, and we were not going there. All else remained the same. I am sure Nurse's relief was great whenever I grew utterly bored and weary and went to sleep.

It would seem that I was asleep when we reached Caer Avalon, for I remember nothing of it except awakening in a real bed in the morning.

The feast began that very morning.

When Nurse led Morgause and me into the great hall, there was the fearsome red-flame-shining dragon flag hanging over the dais, and there lay Mother all gowned in gold satin on a wine red velvet chair such as I had never seen, almost a bed more than a chair, with a fat bald baby in her arms. Above her heavy gown and her necklace of ox-blood stones, her face seemed chalk white; maybe she was sick, and that was why she had to lie down. She put out one arm and hugged me to her and kissed me, and then she let me go and hugged Morgause the same way, but she did not put the baby away; she held him the whole time. "Morgan," she said, her voice as soft as rose petals, "Morgause, you've grown. You're almost young ladies now. Such pretty frocks, such pretty hair. You look lovely."

Morgause said, "Thank you, Mother." I said nothing, only stared at the baby. His round, sleepy face looked almost as red as the velvet chair. He had a white lace dress on. He looked stupid.

Mother bent over him, her pale face very thin compared with his fat one, and kissed him. "It's your baby brother, Morgan," she told me. "Isn't he beautiful?"

"No."

Nurse tapped my head with her knuckles to reprove me. Morgause said, "He's nice."

I felt the fire dragon burning in my chest. Mother should put that ugly baby away and take me in her lap and hold me and kiss me.

Instead, she reached out and smoothed my hair, already escaping from its crown of braids to flop over my forehead.

"Come," Nurse said, leading us away. We did not get to sit near Mother. We sat at a table off to one side, with Nurse between me and Morgause, of course, to keep us from whispering and pinching each other. Uther Pendragon sat by Mother in a golden throne; I wondered whether he kept one here or if he had brought it with him from Caer Argent. I wondered why he was here at Avalon, not in his own court. Was this castle more grand than his? It seemed quite grand, with the vaulted rafters carved and gilded into all sorts of strange things: griffins, fierce winged women, fishtail horses, stars and crescent moons, huge lily flowers. All the tables, even ours, bore white linen cloths broidered with gold, upon which stood sconces of many candles. First I stared at the golden carvings overhead, then the candles, then the many people—lords and ladies they must have been—in finery that made my ruffled blue frock look very plain. Such jewels the ladies wore, although Mother's rubies were the finest. I hoped I would be allowed to wear jewels before I grew too much older. I looked around for other children to see whether they wore finery or jewels, but except for that stupid baby I saw none. Only boring adults sat at my table; there was no one for me to talk with. I watched the candles drip.

After a while a man in red blew a horn, and everyone got silent. Then a lord got up and said things. The edge of my chair was digging into my legs because my feet did not touch the floor. I swung them.

"Sit still," Nurse whispered to me.

It became a very long day.

Once, we all got up and bowed to Uther Pendragon and he stood and said things in his snarly voice and I rubbed the backs of my legs with my hands. Then I had to sit again. Sometimes servants brought things to eat, and some of them were good and some of them were awful but I had to eat some anyway to be polite. I liked the candied quail and the sweetbreads and the apple tarts and the marzipan. I did not like the spiced roast pork. In between things to eat there were tumblers, and I wanted to get up and try to do somersaults too, but I had to sit still. Sometimes the baby cried and Mother drew him up to her bosom and nursed him and I felt the fire dragon hissing in my chest. Sometimes I watched a nurse carry the baby away to diaper him and then bring him back. Sometimes I stared at Uther Pendragon, who never looked at me at all. Mostly I squirmed in my hard chair.

"Shh," Nurse hushed me. "Only a little longer now."

A minstrel in a ragtag tunic stood near the king. From his harp he strummed out a chord that rang like a hundred bells, singing a ballad about True Thomas, who saw a bright lady come riding:

> *Her skirt was of the grass green silk,*
> *Her mantle of the velvet fine,*
> *From every braid of her horse's mane*
> *Hung fifty silver bells and nine.*

She was the queen of Faerie, the otherworld, and she dared him to kiss her, and he did. In my childish mind I never thought otherwise than that the minstrel sang of Thomas the messenger boy I had met. I felt sure that he was true and handsome enough to kiss the queen of Faerie.

And then she told him that he must go with her.

> *She mounted on her milk white steed,*
> *She took True Thomas up behind,*
> *And when she made the bridle ring,*
> *The steed flew swifter than the wind.*

They rode up the ferny hillside, the winding road to Faerie.

> *"Thomas, you must hold your tongue,*
> *Whatever you may hear or see,*
> *For if you speak a word in my land,*
> *You'll never go back to your own country."*

> *On they rode and farther on*
> *And waded through rivers above the knee*
> *And they saw neither sun nor moon,*
> *But they heard the roaring of the sea.*

> *It was dark, dark night with no starlight*
> *And they waded through red blood to the knee,*
> *For all the blood that's shed on earth*
> *Runs through the springs of that country.*

My breath caught, and I did not listen to the rest of the song, for I knew now that my father's blood ran through Faerie. And I knew that it had to be somewhere near where I lived, for they heard the roaring of the sea.

As the last chords rang away, there came shafts of silvergold light from somewhere, from everywhere, and a stir as all those jeweled courtiers turned to look, and—

"The fays!" the herald cried. "Welcome, people of peace!" And he blew a great blast on his golden horn.

They entered through no doorway, from nowhere and everywhere, as if they had been there all along, as if they were made out of foreverness and sun and moon and the light coming out of nowhere, no, coming out of the carved eyes of the

32

golden winged women under the arches, and perhaps I was dreaming.

Uther Pendragon stood up to greet the fays the way we had all stood up before him. Everyone stood. I jumped on top of my chair to try to see.

"Morgan!" Nurse tugged at me.

"Be seated," commanded a sweet young voice. Folk sat, but the king remained standing and I knelt on my chair, gawking. She who had spoken was a barefoot slip of a big-eyed girl, no more than sixteen, with primroses twined in her masses of chestnut hair even though it was long past primrose season. Her shining filmy frock did not cover either her arms or her legs, but she danced up to the high table just so, not caring who saw her. Behind her hobbled a bent, ancient crone supported by a matronly woman not unlike my nurse—but both had the same unearthly sheen as the girl's frock. Her skin and hair, I saw now, glimmered with the same fey light. Her lovely face shone with a subtle glow like starlight. In the middle-aged woman and the ancient one I saw remnants of her eerie beauty.

The three of them progressed past my table on their way to the dais, and I gasped, so struck by surprise that I grabbed at my chair for support: On the left hand of each of them, maiden and matron and ancient crone, shone a silvergold ring, and on each ring I saw just such a stone as the one that hung over my heart. A druid stone. Egg of the world serpent. A milpreve.

I whispered to Nurse, "Are they *goddesses?*"

She gave me a look full of silence.

More fays walked behind those three. I remember a fierce dark woman with the wings of a raven, a brown man with the horns of a stag, a woman who seemed to be all a flow of green water, a snow white man who carried a naked skull in his hands—I grew afraid to look any more. I hid my face against Nurse and listened to the voices.

"How shall the child be named?" It was the maiden's melodious voice.

"He shall be called Arthur," said my mother in a low tone I had never heard from her before. I did not understand the shadow in her voice.

"Arthur," said a fay; it might have been the ancient crone. "Princeling, I gift you with long life."

"Arthur who shall be king, I gift you with dominion," said another.

"Arthur, baby prince, I gift you with strength," said yet another.

"Thank you," murmured my mother's voice.

And so it went on. Courage, manliness, valor in battle. Uther Pendragon had brought Arthur to this place for his name-day just so the fays could come and gift him; Avalon is a magical place, and many such presences dwell there. And it is one of the ways of fays to give gifts to a baby prince. But as I listened, the fire dragon burned in my chest again, and fiercely, fiercely I wished that someday it would be in my power to inflict some ill upon this annoying baby who was a prince and everyone's darling when I was not a princess and nobody was paying any attention to me. I wished it, and I felt my secret stone turn hot against my skin.

"Morgan," said a voice that was not Nurse.

Startled, I straightened and looked. The barefoot girl with primroses in her hair stooped to gaze into my face with laughing green eyes.

"Little oddling-eyed Morgan. And Morgause," she said with a glance at my sister to include her. "And your good nurse." She gifted Nurse with a secret, loving look I did not understand, then turned back to me. "Little Morgan fated to be fate, do you know why you are here?"

Fate again. That word harrowed me with memory of fearsome Merlin, the haunted darkness of his eyes as he had spoken to me that day upon the moor. Whatever fate was, I didn't like it. Dumbly I gazed back at the merry-eyed fay, feeling Nurse's arm creep around me as if to protect me. I felt the snake stone burning against my chest.

"Why are any of us here? For luck for the babe," the half-naked fay answered her own question. Her eyes were like cat eyes shining in firelight, like clover leaves, like green wells. I cowered, and my hand wavered up to cover my chest as if she might somehow see the milpreve under my frock. She smiled. "You're here because it would have been bad luck not to include you," she said. "As if luck matters to fate. Bad luck! Ha! Ha!" She danced away, laughing wildly.

"True love," the matronly fay gifted the baby Arthur.

"Thank you," said my mother in that same low, strained voice, cuddling the sleeping baby in both arms.

I laid my head against Nurse again, closed my eyes and gave up trying to make sense of anything.

The next thing I remember is waking up in the bedchamber. It was dark, and I knew it must be mid of night by the snores of Nurse and others; Morgause and I shared that chamber with a couple of ladies and their maids, for there were many guests to be housed that night at Caer Avalon. Someone besides me was awake, for I heard women's voices whispering.

"Poor Igraine, having to give up her baby."

"And she a queen. But I'd not trade places with her for all the riches—"

"No, not I either. Three months she's nursed that babe at her own breast—"

"And where is it to go? Is some other woman to give up her babe now to nurse this one?"

"It's a hard, hard thing to be a woman, queen or no."

I felt wide awake—no wonder, as I had been sleeping for hours. And my eyes were making sense of the darkness now; I could see my way to the door. Softly I slipped from my bed and pattered out, my bare feet cold on the drafty floor. Whoever they were, talking, either they did not see me go or did not care.

I did not know where my mother's chamber was in this place, or why I wanted to find it—perhaps only to stare on mystery as before.

I wandered stony corridors at random. Once I heard the scuttling of a mouse, and once I sensed the swoop of a bat, but I saw no folk, heard no—

I stiffened and stopped where I was.

Somewhere, someone was crying. A woman. Sobbing, but choking back the sound. No one was supposed to hear.

Something swept down the corridor toward me.

It was so much like a huge darkness moving in, like storm clouds over the sea, that I froze a moment before I understood that it was a man. Then I heard his heavy footfalls, saw his starry, shadowy floating robes. I shrank against the wall, and Merlin, massive in his hooded mantle, strode past me with the

36

blanket-wrapped baby in his arms. He did not look at me, but I saw his face, for on his forehead, above the terrifying blackness of his eyes, he wore a luminous band. And centered on that band shone a stone I recognized at once.

Long after he had passed I stood there trembling.

4

MANY YEARS PASSED BEFORE I SAW MY MOTHER again, far from Caer Tintagel.

I lost my home when I was twelve years old.

I remember that day well. At the time Nurse was trying to teach me how to spin, and I was sulkily at it in the solarium, producing yards of lumpy thread, when I heard the ring of cantering hooves on the cobbles of the courtyard. I jumped onto my chair so that I could see out the window, and my heart leaped: It was Thomas, on Annie.

I had seen him only a few times since that day he had fetched me down from the quoit stone and given me a pony ride. But I had not forgotten.

Instead, I forgot spinning forthwith. I ran out the door—"Morgan, where are you going?" Morgause called after me from the loom. Without answering I dashed down the spiral stairs to the courtyard. Thomas had already gone in to the steward with his message, but Annie stood steaming at the hitching ring. I did not mind her sweaty hide; I patted and patted her sweet gray face and arranged her forelock between her eyes. She nuzzled me, and I patted her sleek wet neck and stroked her mane.

Footsteps. I turned, ready to resist anyone who might try to drag me away from the pony, but then I forgot all about Annie. It was Thomas.

He was taller than before, but then, so was I. And he was still the Thomas I remembered, a lightweight message rider, not yet a man, his face not yet a man's face; it was the face of an angel. I was no longer young and silly enough to think that he had been to Faerie, but I still felt that in some way he was True Thomas.

"Lady Morgan," he said. He remembered me.

"I'm no lady yet," I said, instantly hating myself; why did the wrong words always spill out of my mouth? I did not want him to find out what a beast I could be. "Thomas," I added lamely, trying to soften the rude edge.

He smiled, but there was something very dark and worried in his sky blue eyes. He stood close to me and in a low voice he said, "Uther Pendragon is dead."

I was surprised, but I cared nothing for Uther Pendragon, so the news meant little to me. I was not yet old enough to understand the import of what he said.

But I heard a gasp behind me. I turned, and there stood Nurse, no doubt come to fetch me back to my spinning.

"How so?" she whispered. Her face looked like snow upon a boulder.

Thomas looked at her as if deciding whether to speak on, then spoke, keeping his voice very low. "He sickened and died. Two days ago."

"What—what is to become of Queen Igraine?"

I stiffened, for—what was Nurse saying? That my mother might be in danger? I looked to Thomas for an answer. But he gave no answer. He only gazed back at Nurse with that shadow in his eyes.

Nurse asked, "Who sent you here?"

"Uther's seneschal."

"The seneschal? Does he now claim the throne?"

Thomas did an odd thing. Instead of answering, he peered over his shoulder toward the steps of the keep, where peasants waited to go in and plead their cases before Redburke, the turnip-nosed steward. And then he looked upward, to where the sky blew low and gray over the walls of Tintagel.

In the sky wheeled a great bird the color of darkest dead ashes, its motionless wings wider than those of an eagle. Beside me, I heard Nurse's heavy breathing catch. "The Morrigun," she said, almost choking.

"What?" I asked.

Thomas lowered his sky blue gaze to me, but no one answered. There was a long silence. I stood there staring back at him without comprehension. "What *is* it?" I demanded finally.

He whispered so softly I barely heard him. "The Morrigun is flying."

"There will be war," Nurse said in a crushed voice. "Men are fated to die."

Fate again. I hated fate. What was this meddlesome fate

that it should concern me? Fate had better let me alone. "War? Where?" I demanded.

His voice low, Thomas told me, "Everywhere, most likely. There are many who will wish to be king."

I began to understand, but only insofar as it concerned him. "What will you do? Where will you go?"

"I don't know."

I heard a ladylike rustling of skirts and turned to find Morgause standing beside me. I tried not to scowl, but all I could think was that Thomas might like Morgause better than me, for Morgause was a sweet, shy violet of a young lady, mannerly, soft-spoken, everything I was not.

With an abrupt change of tone, as if we had been discussing nothing more than social pleasantries all along, Nurse asked Thomas, "Will you stop here tonight?"

"Yes. Annie must rest."

"I'll find you a pallet, then."

"No need." He gave her a long look. "I'll make myself a bed of straw in the stable."

Nurse nodded, beckoned to Morgause and me, and led us inside, back to work.

"Who was that?" Morgause asked.

Nurse seemed not to hear. Morgause spoke so softly and gently, always, that she was accustomed to not being heard. She did not ask again.

At the door of the solarium, Nurse touched my elbow to hold me back while Morgause entered.

"Morgan," Nurse murmured to me, "not a word. Our lives depend on it." She gave me a look that took me in with a power I had not known was in her. Her eyes shone like the laughing fay's that fearsome time at Avalon, like cat eyes gleaming in firelight. Shimmering clover green. Like falling into a deep, tree-shaded well. Was this—Nurse? My stolid, familiar nurse, with such unaccountable green power in her? It seemed so. Her gaze enchanted me and terrified me for a flashing moment before she turned away and led me back to my spinning.

Perhaps an hour later I sensed someone watching me and looked up to see Redburke, of all people, looming in the doorway. Certainly he had never before taken such an interest in Morgause and me and our industry at the wheel and loom, but there he stood, all six broad burly feet of him, scowling out of his bearish hairy face at both of us. Morgause gazed blankly back at him, then ducked her chin in maidenly confusion. I merely stared like the rude child I was. Nurse stood up, curtsied, and said in her flat country way, "Your servant, Lord Steward. You wish something?"

"Bah," he growled, and he went away.

That night I could not sleep for thinking of Annie and Thomas, Thomas and Nurse, Nurse and the potent caution she had laid on me, and Redburke, and Uther Pendragon dead and Mother and Thomas again, round and round, a glimmering green eddy of thoughts swirling ever back to Thomas until I grew tired of lying still.

But when I slipped from my bed to go wandering, my snoring nurse, without breaking the rhythm of her drone, reached up from her pallet and seized me by the arm to stop me. I was so surprised I squeaked.

"Shhh." She sat up, and even in the dark I could see that she was not wearing her nightshirt. Instead of being a white blur, she looked like a shadow. Under her blanket she was wearing her daytime clothes. "Dress," she whispered to me. Then she stood up and joggled my sister. "Morgause. Come, get up. Dress."

She reached into our chests of clothing and without searching, as if she had laid out everything earlier, she handed us what we were to wear: warm wool stockings, our plainest brown frocks, shawls, mantles, stout shoes. While we struggled to dress in the dark, she pulled out from under her bedclothes bags already packed full of we knew not what. She handed us each one to carry and took two herself. "Have you your stone?" she murmured to me.

I pressed my hand to the front of my dress and nodded.

"Very well. Follow me. Not a sound," she cautioned, and she led us out of the chamber.

By back ways, motioning us to tread softly, she led us through the kitchen and the scullery and the creamery and the mews to the stable. These were not places where we commonly went. Maids slumbered by the hearth in the kitchen. Hooded hawks slept erect, one foot pulled up to their breasts, on the perches in the mews. All was shadow and mystery, as always when I wandered the night, but this time I was not alone, and my heart pulsed hard with wonder: Where was Nurse taking us? Her silent power made me mind her for once, so that I walked like the others, slowly, slowly, careful not to knock into anything. Above the sound of our own breathing we could hear the footsteps of guards in the courtyard, but no one saw us as we slipped into the stable.

43

It smelled warmly of straw and horse in there, and I heard the flutter of nostrils and the thud of a hoof as someone's hot-tempered charger stirred in its stall. Dim orange light filtered in from torches burning in their sconces on the courtyard walls. In that light I saw—

"Thomas!"

I did not say it loudly, but Nurse dropped her bags and clapped her hand over my mouth, pinching my shoulder hard with her other hand.

"Shh, Morgan," breathed Thomas, his tone gentle. He picked up the bags, looped them together by the handles and slung them over Annie's rump; there stood the little gray mare saddled and bridled and looking as fresh as morning. Waiting for us.

"Girls on her?" Thomas whispered to Nurse.

She must have nodded, because Thomas took my bag and set it aside, grasped me by the waist, lifted me and swung me onto Annie, seating me sideward in the saddle. "Swing one foot over her neck," he whispered, and I did so, bunching my skirts around my knees, wide-eyed with the glory of being perched high and astride. Nurse helped him hoist my sister up behind me; Morgause clung to me around my waist as if I might somehow protect her from all this strangeness. Without a word Nurse picked up the bags we had been carrying and Thomas took Annie by the reins. Nurse and Thomas looked at each other.

Nurse motioned with her head and walked out the big stable door. Thomas followed her, and Annie followed Thomas.

My heart pounded, and I could not think. Riding Annie, astride, in the dark of night—the king had died, and now something huge was happening. Something midnight hidden, something Redburke must not know. Where were we going?

Laden by baggage, Nurse trudged across the courtyard to the gates, and—now what? There were guards at the gates. They would send us straight to Redburke.

"Halt! Who—"

"Open the gates," Nurse said in that flat way of hers.

Her female voice brought a sentry out of the gatehouse to look at her. He scanned us all and grinned. "Woman, are you moon-mad? Where do you think—"

Nurse gave him such a look as she had given me earlier that day, the fey green gaze that had kept me from saying to anyone, even to Morgause, what I had heard. I saw her eyes flash green, like the flash of a salmon just under the surface of a wave, and I shivered.

"Open the gates," Nurse told him, and without another word, dumbly like Morgause's muslin doll, he turned and began to crank up the portcullis. The wheel creaked, the chain rattled, and other guards came running down.

"What—"

"Open the gates," Nurse commanded them. Her back was to me, so I did not see her eyes. But the same green power must have been in her, for their eyes widened, their mouths closed, and they obeyed. They spread the gates wide.

We issued out in silence. I heard the gates close behind me, but I did not look back. Morgause hid her head against the back of my shoulder and began silently to sob.

In that moment I felt a chill in the marrow of my bones, a sure sense that my life had utterly changed.

◆ ◆ ◆

Under a vast, cold indigo sky we wound our way up the moors, past quoit stones and tall upright stones that stood like shadowy giants in the night. I drew my mantle close over my chest and felt glad of Morgause's warm presence at my back. She had ceased crying, but no one spoke.

Finally in a low voice Thomas said, "Protector, by what title am I to address you?"

Nurse turned to him and said gently enough, "By my name."

I must have been quite stupid as a child. It had never occurred to me that Nurse had a name.

But she did not tell it to us. We plodded on in darkness and silence.

Thomas hazarded, "Ongwynn?"

She turned to him as if to an equal. "Yes. How did you know, Thomas?"

"I—I don't know. I don't know anything."

"But you do. You know much."

Ongwynn? It was not a name I had ever heard. Who was Ongwynn? And who was Thomas, that he knew of her?

Morgause must have felt as bewildered as I did. From just behind my ear her voice quavered, "Nurse?"

"Yes?"

"Where are we going?"

"To my home."

It had never occurred to me that Nurse had a home either. Morgause whimpered, "But—but why?"

Nurse slogged on without answering. I told Morgause, "Because Uther Pendragon is dead." Somehow it was now permissible for me to say this.

"*What?*"

Thomas reached over to take one of the bags from Nurse—from Ongwynn, rather. As he walked, he spoke over his shoulder to Morgause and me. "The king is dead. His lords and stewards will want to seize his lands. Your sons, if you have sons, will be the rightful heirs of Cornwall. Anyone who wants to claim Cornwall will try to kill you or imprison you."

Including, no doubt, Redburke. We had survived this long because he did not know we knew. He had no reason to think that Thomas would tell us. Thomas was our protector, I realized, as much as Nurse was.

No, her name was not Nurse. It was Ongwynn.

Without turning Ongwynn said, "Uther Pendragon would have slain you before now if it were not for your mother."

I felt my breath stop. I sat on Annie with my mouth open, gulping like a fish.

Morgause asked, her voice bleakly calm now, "We—we are not going home again?"

No one answered.

I found my breath again, and started babbling, "The—the rings Mother gave us, the rings made of her hair—"

Ongwynn said, "I have them. Hush."

I hushed. I thought of dolls, two red, heart-shaped pincushions, favorite frocks, things left behind. I looked back over my shoulder, but it was too late; Caer Tintagel was far out of sight in the night.

We traveled until dawn, then took shelter under the shadow of a lonely dolmen—three standing stones with a great flat slab laid atop them like a roof. A place made by a giant's hand, no one knew why. No one came to such places customarily. Out of one of the bags Ongwynn gave us bread and cheese to eat, and water from a flask. Then we slept, huddled together for warmth on the chill shale.

Late in the day we awoke, stiff and bone-cold, ate a little and moved on.

The days and nights of that journey have blurred together in my memory into chill, dark, weariness and little more. We traveled mostly toward the North Star; Thomas pointed it out to me one clear night, and showed me how the little bear and the big bear danced around it, and from far across the sky the giant raised his arrow to take aim at them both. But most nights were neither clear nor starlit, and we stumbled through them. We slipped around villages in the dead of night, hid behind hedges by day. Ongwynn walked ever more slowly, I did not know why—I did not then understand how much her use of the green power had cost her. Perhaps it had even cost her her good sense. Thomas tried to say that Morgause and I should walk and Ongwynn should ride, but she would not hear of it. She plodded on. Thomas taught me to guide Annie by the reins so that he could take both bags from Ongwynn. I grew saddle-sore. We were drenched by rain. Morgause and I grew quarrelsome, then sullen and mute. Somewhere Thomas found us a few eggs; we gulped them raw. We spoke little.

"What will happen to my mother?" I asked one silent night.

Thomas looked at me but did not answer. Ongwynn did not turn her head, only trudged on for so long that I thought there would be no answer. When she finally spoke, it was like hearing a voice from the wind. "Whoever claims the throne will also claim the queen."

"Likely she has fled somewhere," Thomas said, low.

Morgause laid her forehead against the back of my neck but for once she did not cry. We were toughening, both of us, beyond crying.

Or so I thought.

One dawn as we cast about for a place to hide during the day we blundered upon the aftermath of a battle.

The carrion birds were gathering, crows and ravens and black vultures—I shivered at the sight of the vultures, wheeling like omens, like the larger omen I had seen wheeling over Tintagel, the Morrigun. The swarming of the birds should have warned us off; the stench alone should have kept Ongwynn from leading us there. Perhaps she was too weary to notice or care. Or perhaps she wanted Morgause and me to see. There was war everywhere, as Thomas had said, and it was well for us to understand what war meant.

Remains lay in a twisted mess like wrack and jellyfish on the shore after a storm. The victors, whoever they were, had looted the defeated and also mutilated some of them. I saw headless bodies. I saw a dead man naked from the waist down, a strange, pale, bloated form, like some sort of awful fruit abandoned amid vines. Rising like a scarecrow over that dreadful garden stood a lance, its butt wedged through a tall man's ribs into the ground, and on its tip his severed head—I supposed it had been his. He had been a goodly, bearded man. Now he was a horror with his face slashed open, his eyes and nose eaten away.

Morgause said quite calmly, "That is what they did to our father."

Until that moment, no matter how many times they told me Daddy was dead, I had not fully understood.

I did not cry then. But later, when we had found a river hollow to hide in, I could not sleep. I crept away from the others and ran back the way we had come, back toward the stench and the wheeling black cloud of crows and ravens and vultures in the sky.

I got no farther than a copse of alder trees near the edge of the battlefield. There I stumbled across a body lying facedown, fully clothed, like a person sleeping except for the dark stain on his back. He had tried to run away, perhaps. Or he had crawled here to die. He was a small, slim man, not much bigger than a boy.

I backed away without touching him, and then I lay in the dead, dirty brown alder leaves on the ground and wept.

I had not been there long before Thomas found me. He walked silently; I did not realize he was there until he grasped me by the shoulders and lifted me, but I knew his gentle touch at once. "Come on," he murmured, "before Ongwynn misses you."

I stood, but I clung to him and wept against his shoulder. He stood there, stroked my back as if he were patting Annie, and said nothing.

I flung back my head, peering fiercely at his beautiful face through my tears, and I cried, "It must not happen to you."

His azure gaze turned to answer me. He said, his tone as bleak and gray as the sky, "It's likely to. When I was born, the midwife told my mother I was fated to die in battle."

Fate be damned. I felt the secret stone burn on my chest. I cried, "No. No! Never. It must not be."

BOOK TWO

Caer Ongwynn

5

HALF AWAKE AT DAWN, I DREAMED I WAS HOME
again in Tintagel, for I could hear the roaring of the sea.

I sighed, stretched, and realized that I lay not in my eiderdown bed but on a heap of straw under a domed roof of stone.
Home, yes, but not Tintagel.

Ongwynn's home.

Just the nightfall before, we had dragged in, too weary to
notice much or care. Now I sat up to look around me. Peach-
colored dawn light and a waft of chill dawn air drifted in
through narrow half-moon openings in the rough stone walls,
squat arches veiled in heather and ivy. Beside me on the straw,
swaddled in her mantle as I was in mine, sleeping in her frock
as I had slept in mine, Morgause turned her head away from
the light, murmured and slept on.

I felt exhausted enough to do the same. But I knew Thomas
had been up half the night with Ongwynn. I pressed my lips together, rubbed the sleep out of my eyes, staggered to my bare

feet and padded off through this wild, rude fortress to find them.

Not a fortress, exactly, but a—a bastion, a haven, a hiding place. A secret stronghold in the stony bosom of earth herself. A hollow hill.

Not large enough to be called a fortress either. There were a few sleeping chambers, that was all, honeycombed around a larger chamber with a great stone fireplace. By the hearth Thomas sat nodding, his head on his knees, but the fire burned warmly; not too long ago he had piled on more peat. At his feet, lying on a bed made of everything soft we could find to pile there, wrapped in her mantle and Thomas's as well, lay Ongwynn.

Thomas lifted his head as I walked toward him, although barefoot I made almost no noise. "Get shoes on," he whispered. "You'll catch cold."

Perverse, as always, I ignored his order and sat beside him. The hearth fire would warm my feet. "How is she?"

He leaned forward and touched Ongwynn's forehead without speaking, smoothing back her sandy hair grizzled with gray. He did not answer me. The fact that she did not feel his touch was answer enough.

"Go get some sleep," I murmured. "I'll watch." I could feed peat and whitethorn sticks to the fire as well as he, bathe her hot brow as well as he could. How odd for me to be nursing Nurse. Everything had changed.

Thomas shook his head. "I have to check on Annie." He had left his beloved little mare outside, hobbled, to graze. But although he spoke of Annie, he did not move. Too weary. We both sat there, lulled by the warmth of the fire.

"Thomas?" I whispered.

He turned his head to me.

I asked what I had never dared to ask in Nurse's presence. "Thomas, who is she? Who is Ongwynn?"

The silence stretched so long that I thought he would not answer. When he spoke he kept his voice as soft as a breath of summer breeze. "She is to whom commoners pray."

I gasped. "A goddess?"

"Shhh." Some things were not to be spoken of so rashly. "No. She's more of a—a wise woman, a good witch—"

"A fay? But she doesn't wear—" I stopped short, my telltale hand flying to my chest.

Thomas gave me a small, tired smile. "It's no secret that there's something magical about you, Morgan."

That frightened me. He knew of the milpreve; did he also know of the fearsome stirrings within me, darkness and fire? And—magic? I knew nothing of magic. I stammered, "What—how so?"

But Thomas said nothing of the stone at all. He said, "Your eyes."

I sat speechless.

Thomas gazed at me. "Your eyes," he said softly, "like violets at midnight, velvet green and—and porphyry. The Gypsies say—" He stopped.

"What?" I whispered.

He looked at the floor now. "A colt with one brown eye and one blue is elf ridden," he said, giving each word a quiet weight. "A baby with such eyes—a changeling. You—" His glance flashed up to my face and he smiled—his smile took my breath away. "You, who knows? Are you a changeling, Morgan? A visitor from Faerie?"

His tone was so warm and whimsical that his words added only a little to my fear. "I—I don't think so!"

Thomas had mercy on me. "Maybe I have listened to too many firelit tales."

Near our feet, Ongwynn shifted her shoulders as if they hurt from some burden, murmuring something as she stirred. I leaned over to stroke her coarse grizzled hair, like a gray horse's mane, away from her forehead. I would not mind being like Ongwynn, I considered. I asked Thomas, "Is she indeed a fay?"

"No, I think she is what you would call a pedlar, a white witch. Likely she knows spells for easy birthing and to heal clubfoot, leprosy, colic, that sort of thing. And we've seen that she knows something of the old powers."

"But . . ." It seems laughable now, but his calm listing of a pedlar's powers awed me at the time. "But what more can a fay do?"

"I don't know."

"But you say—"

"All I know is . . ." He stopped to think, then spoke softly. "Pedlars are like the rest of us, they grow old and weaken and die. But fays—stay."

"Fays live forever?"

"In a way." He frowned, for these were deep matters, and he spoke slowly. "They—they take different forms . . . and they are like the cycle of seasons, or like the moon; they wax and wane. They have dwindled somewhat since the old golden days. But they will grow strong again."

"Different forms? They change shapes?"

"I—I have heard so, Morgan, but how can I know? I am just a commoner. Fays are for noble folk such as you."

"You're no commoner," I declared. No one could look at him and think him a commoner.

He lowered his gaze. After a moment he said, "I have cast in my lot with commoners." Then, probably to turn me away from more questions, he looked at me and said, "See if you can't get some kind of soup cooking for her, would you?" He got up, stumbling with weariness, and left to see to Annie.

Soup. Soup for Ongwynn.

I had never touched a cooking pot in my life. But the journey had turned me from a coddled girl to nearly a woman within a fortnight, and I set about doing what I could. Pegged to the chimney walls hung odds and ends of cookware, knives and pokers and such. I found an iron kettle and dragged it out through the portal—I cannot properly call it a doorway, for it was like slipping through a quoit stone, a hole in the stony hillside, hidden amid gorse bushes. This was a secret place, Ongwynn's home, with the sea washing against rocky shores on three sides and no village anywhere near. Halfway up the hillside behind Ongwynn's dwelling, the spring flowed from a rocky scarp into a pool where fallow deer and foxes drank, where willow and rowan grew. In their green shadow, silver trout swam with barely a ripple. Standing amid rushes, a bittern lifted its head as I dipped my kettle full of water, and a bittern is the most wild of waterbirds, but this one did not take flight. There was an ancient green magic in this place, giving it great peace.

I wanted to stay by the spring, even though my bare feet

shivered in the dewy heather, but I needed to take care of Ongwynn. Lugging the water back inside, I spilled some on myself and grew truly cold. As I hung the kettle on the hook over the fire, Ongwynn stirred and groaned.

I knelt beside her and soothed her hot forehead with my cold, wet hand. She opened her eyes and gazed at me.

"I'm trying to make you some soup," I told her.

Her lips moved. "I need . . ." But her voice was like the sighing of a sea wind. I could not make out the words.

"What, Nurse? What do you need?"

Her gaze clouded. She closed her eyes.

"It sounded like scone. Rude scone, or something like that," said my sister's voice. I looked up to see Morgause standing over me, sleepy-eyed, her hair tangled and riddled with straw, as I am sure mine was also. "Morgan, you're soaking wet. Your feet are blue with cold."

I did not bark and snarl at her as I would once have done. While I still scorned her as the mouse she was, during the long days of riding I had realized that I needed her.

"Go put on stockings and shoes," she said.

"In a minute." I turned to check on the fire. It burned strongly enough. "What goes in soup?"

"Meat and barley and leeks and such."

Oh, certainly. And a roast suckling pig and a fresh roe-filled salmon or two. "Where shall we get"—I mimicked her voice—"meat and barley and leeks and such?"

Morgause shrugged. "I'll look around. You go find dry clothes."

There were few enough clothes to share amid the pair of us, all of them in sore need of washing. Shivering in the chill of our straw-piled bedchamber, rummaging in our bags, it took me a while to find something dry and only moderately filthy to put on. When I got back to the warmth of the hearth, there at the rude table to one side of the fireplace sat Morgause placidly chopping carrots and parsnips and something brown—dried meat.

Dried meat! "Where did you get that?" I exclaimed.

"In the pantry." Morgause slipped a bit of carrot into her mouth. "Mmm. Sweet. Nice and fresh."

I grabbed an orange circle. "Why would there be fresh carrots in the pantry?" I mumbled around my own chewing. Ongwynn's home had the feel of having been empty for years. It was a cave, for the love of mercy. A hollow tor echoing with the roar of the sea. That sound of grumbling salt water, and the salt air I breathed, made me feel at home here, but in truth this place was not much like Tintagel. No busy comings and goings. No folk. Not a cottage in sight. "Does someone know we are here?" I reached for a whole carrot, but Morgause snatched it away from me.

"Don't. We need it for the soup. That's all there is."

Behind me I heard a surprised breath. I turned. Thomas stood staring, a few wild onions dangling in his hand.

"Where—" he whispered.

"In the pantry," Morgause said at the same time I did.

Thomas took a long breath and lifted his head, turning toward the morning light. He scanned the domed and groined hall of stone. I looked to see what he was looking for and saw nothing but rock, dust, cobwebs and shadows. Yet Thomas spoke. "Thank you, dwellers in Caer Ongwynn," he said softly to the shadows.

Caer Ongwynn? This was no castle.

Yet no one laughed.

Except, perhaps, the denizens. From somewhere there sounded a kind of squeak or chuckle—it might have been a hedgehog or some sort of bird. I wanted to think it was just a bird or a mouse that had come in from outside.

Morgause and I looked at each other. Neither of us spoke. She turned back to slicing parsnips.

On her makeshift bed Ongwynn stirred and murmured.

"Has she come to herself at all?" Thomas asked.

I nodded. "Just for a moment. She said something I couldn't quite catch."

"Something about bread," Morgause said.

"Scone," I corrected, for a scone was not quite the same thing as bread.

"Bread would be better for her," Morgause said.

"What does it matter? Scone or bread, we do not have it to give to her."

The water in the kettle had finally started to steam, although it was not yet boiling. Morgause scooped up handfuls of chopped dried meat and plunked them in, then the vegetables. Wobbling with weariness, Thomas nudged peat into the fire.

"Thomas," I told him, "go sleep."

"I'm not tired," he said, and he sat down on the stone floor near Ongwynn. Glancing at him a moment later, I saw that his head drooped, eyes closed.

"You're going to fall over and conk yourself," I told him.

He did not answer, but began to sag to one side. I could have bowled him over with a touch. The thought tempted me and made me smile, but I took him by the shoulders and eased him to the stone, where he sprawled and slumbered. I stood gazing at him. Many folk look more beautiful, more innocent, more holy when they are sleeping, but Thomas did not. It was not possible. He had about him the innocent courage of a holy hero always.

"Morgan," Morgause said to me.

I turned to her. She had left the soup to tend itself and knelt dabbing Ongwynn's forehead with the wet corner of her shawl.

I knelt beside her. "Is she any better?"

"No."

She sat on the floor by Nurse—Ongwynn—and I sat beside her, staring at the sick woman as she did.

Just a common, blocky, sandy-haired Cornishwoman.

"There is so much I do not understand," Morgause murmured. "This is her home? A hollow hill, a spirit grange? How did such a one come to us?"

I said nothing, but I shared her wondering. Why had Ongwynn, pedlar to whom all commoners prayed, become our nurse?

Wondering was no use. I stood up. "Come on," I told Morgause.

"Where?"

"Just—looking."

I hauled her to her feet. Hand in hand we tiptoed through Ongwynn's home, peering into the shadows of the half-moon arches, the vines, the groins, the niches in the stone walls. Our wanderings took us to our bedchamber, where we let go of each other long enough to grab our mantles and trot back to Thomas and bundle them around him as he slept. We checked on Ongwynn, then set off snooping again. We found a chamber stacked with heavy wooden chests, and we tried to look into one, leaving our finger marks in its dust; although we saw no padlock, we could not pry open the lid. In another chamber we saw, standing all alone in the middle of the stone floor, a golden goblet fit for a king, so glowing even through its dust that we did not dare to go near it. Other than those things, we found nothing out of the way—a root cellar, empty; the hollow of a baking oven behind the fireplace; a few rotting wooden water buckets. A pink-footed mouse or two scampered away from us. A dove cooed then flew over our heads. We saw no signs of any other life but these and ourselves.

Yet when we reached the pantry—a cubbyhole carved into the stone—there laid out on dock leaves sat bread, a dozen little loaves the size of our fists, freshly baked.

Morgause took the first watch over Ongwynn that night, and I the second. We had lifted Ongwynn and tried to feed her soup and bread, but we had not succeeded in getting much of it into her. Sometimes she shook with cold even by the hearth fire, and other times she sweated and burned with fever, and she had not come to herself all day.

My belly was full of good food, the best I had tasted in weeks, yet I felt empty. Alone in the mid of night, I sat by Ongwynn, kept the hearth fire going, and tried not to think or feel much.

Father, gone. Then, Mother. Now—Nurse?

And here I sat in a benighted cave instead of Tintagel. I began to understand that I could depend on nothing in my life. Nothing.

Except myself.

I had loved my father, and he was dead.

Mother . . . where was Mother now?

Nurse . . .

Soft footsteps, and here came Thomas to join me—early, it seemed to me. He sat beside me at the hearth, but I did not move from my place.

"I'll watch," he told me. "Go sleep."

I shook my head. I could not possibly have slept. A voice, my own, said like a ghost in the night, "She's going to die."

Thomas did not dispute it. He sat silent.

From around the corner of the fireplace, where we had left a food offering upon a dock leaf as Thomas had advised, there came small sounds such as squirrels might have made: rustle, squeak, chuckle. I startled, and would have jumped up to look, but Thomas put his hand on my shoulder to restrain me.

"Blessed earth folk," he said softly to the night, "can you help Ongwynn?"

The sounds ceased. Only silence answered him.

He let go of my shoulder. "I should not have asked," he murmured. "Now I've distressed them."

I whispered, "How do you know?"

"They have only small powers. Make a flower bloom, mend a shoe, cozen a butterfly. And you should not overtax them, or they can be mischievous."

"No, I mean—how do you know such things?"

"It makes sense that Ongwynn would have such folk about her."

What he took for sense I saw as far more. "No! I mean . . ." I shook my head like Annie shaking off flies and asked of him the question he had once asked Ongwynn. "Who are you?"

Silence.

"Thomas?"

He said gently—almost always he spoke gently—"You'll be safer if I do not tell you."

"But—"

He leaned forward, elbows on his knees, shoulders hunched, looking at the floor. "Uther Pendragon killed my father," he said, "and my mother and my two little sisters, much as he would have killed you if it had suited him."

His voice was so quiet and calm that it harrowed me more than tears would have. I whispered, "I'm sorry."

He nodded but did not look at me. "It was all a muddle of darkness and blood and fire and—and screams," he said. "Men-at-arms took hold of me and hit me until it was nothing but black. When I awoke I was in a dungeon." He shuddered and stopped speaking.

"I'm sorry," I whispered again.

"Death is kinder than prison," Thomas said, low. "I watched my father die in his shackles before they killed him."

"I—" I did not understand. "Did they starve him?"

"Of course." He gave me a glance that almost pitied me, then looked to the stone floor again. "His manhood died, I mean. Prison slew his soul. When they took him out to kill him, he had no heart left, no good-bye for me."

I thought I understood. "I miss my father too."

He said nothing.

I asked, "Why did they let you go?"

"They didn't. They dragged me to the block in my turn, but I was little and skinny as an eel, they had no chains that would not fall off me, and somehow I wiggled out of their grasp. I ran into the forest."

I had been thinking of him as always and forever a handsome youth. "You were just a little boy?"

He nodded. "In my seventh summer. Not quite old enough to make a proper outlaw." He lifted his head with a wry smile, trying to joke, but neither of us laughed. "I wandered and wept and tried to find something to eat, but I was already so starved I had no strength to fend for myself. I lay down to die. When I awoke, Gypsies were feeding me."

"Gypsies!"

He nodded. "Annie is a Gypsy pony."

"They—they raised you?"

"Yes. They took me in and cherished me and beat me when I needed it and told me their stories and taught me to be a horseman."

"Nobody should beat you! Not ever!"

He looked at me, smiling; he could smile now, being past the sorrowful part. "A beating is nothing compared to . . ." He let the thought go.

Compared to being slaughtered by a conquering king? Compared to dying in battle? Compared to his fate?

"But I could not stay a Gypsy," he said. "They steal. I can't steal. Something in me won't let me."

True Thomas.

"When I was old enough I thanked them and left them and journeyed to Caer Argent to serve Uther Pendragon."

The king who had killed his family? *"Why?"*

Thomas said just as gently as ever, "I meant to learn all I

could of him. I meant to be trusted by him. And then, when I was a man and strong enough, I meant to take my revenge."

At our feet, Ongwynn stirred and groaned. I knelt by her side, dipped the kerchief in the pan of cool water we had placed nearby and bathed her face. Her breathing panted, shallow, and she did not open her eyes to look at me.

"Fate has seen fit to save me from being a murderer," Thomas murmured.

I did not like what Thomas was saying. I did not like to think that he could kill. And he spoke of fate, and I did not understand or like the ways of fate. Blast fate, if it wanted to take Uther Pendragon, why couldn't it have done so before he had killed my father? And what did fate want Nurse for, when I needed her? That laughing fay had said I was fated to be fate? Nonsense. Idiocy. If fate wanted Nurse to die, I had to fight it any way I could.

I cupped Ongwynn's head in my hands, lifted it and demanded, "Nurse, tell me what will make you well."

She did not answer. She did not see me. Her eyes opened but they were only shadows in her face, as blind as if they had been picked out by crows. I meant nothing to her anymore.

I shook her. "Answer me!"

I felt Thomas take hold of my shoulders, tugging me away from her. "Morgan, she can't."

I twisted loose of his hold, staying where I was, kneeling beside Ongwynn. All fate be damned, what was it that she had said? I was not at all convinced that stupid Morgause had heard her correctly. Rude scone?

"Scone," I whispered, puzzling aloud, "spoon, stone, crude stone, good stone, trued stone—"

"Morgan," breathed Thomas, his voice taut. I looked up at him, and he stood like a deer about to leap, his eyes wide, gazing at me.

Druid stone.

Even before I thought it, my hand, which often seemed to have more sense than my head, pressed to my chest. Against my skin I could feel the stone burning like my own fury against fate.

Despite that fire I froze, icy with fear. Terror. Magic? Something magical about me? But I knew nothing of magic, and I remembered the black pits that were Merlin's eyes. What might happen to me if I attempted this fearsome thing?

Yet I had to try.

My hand found the red silk cord knotted around my neck. I drew the druid stone out of my frock and let it swing free and naked in the firelight. In that flickering tawny glow, the milpreve shone with its own fey sky blue–gold light, pulsing like an azure star, a cold spark so bright it made me blink. I heard Thomas gasp, but I did not speak to him; I sensed that I had better waste neither time nor strength talking. I took the fey stone in the palm of my left hand, where it burned blue, blue. With my right hand I pulled the covers back from Nurse. Then my hand hovered over her until, with its own good sense, it came to rest on her chest just where her old brown dress opened into collar, where her breastbone widened at the base of her neck, close to her heart. I pressed my hand into the warmth that had cared for me from birth and whispered, "Please."

I could feel the life fluttering too weak in her humble neck. Other than that, nothing happened.

"Please," I said to the night, the stone shining true blue and relentless in the darkness. "I need her."

Nothing. Not even a chuckle in the shadows.

Then, like the brat I was, like the mule-headed child she had raised me to be, I flared into rage because I was not getting my own way. "A pox on you!" I shouted at the night, at the distant, darkened moon, sending echoes and doves flying; I could hear beating wings and frightened whistlings overhead. "Damn everything!" And in that tantrum moment I somehow knew what I had to say, what I had to surrender. I yelled, "All right, I am Morgan and I am fey, damn it, and I will be—I will be whatever I have to be to save her! Blast it, now make her well!"

Even after all these many years, I do not understand much better than I did then whence the power comes or where it goes. All I know is that it knocks me about as badly as any beating I care to imagine. It walloped me like a blow from Uther Pendragon's mailed fist, like a quoit stone thrown at my head, like a whack from a not-so-playful giant, like being hurled off a cliff into the sea, thrown into a dungeon by huge enemies. All in an instant, not enough time to flee or even to move—but in that instant I felt Nurse move under my hand. I felt the great veins of her neck pulse strongly. I felt her start to sit up, and I heard her blessed voice exclaim my name—and then darkness. I knew nothing more.

6

THOMAS WENT AWAY ONLY A FEW DAYS LATER.

I had lain a day abed, weak and dazed, and then I was all right, although bruised. I hobbled when I walked, and Ongwynn said my face looked tragic, all great black eyes. She made much of me, everyone made much of me, and I gladly let them; it felt wonderful to be cosseted and praised. And it was all because I had dared to attempt magic. That power had made me a heroine. Ongwynn felt as well and strong as when she was twenty, she said. Better than before we left Tintagel.

That day, the day Thomas left, started like a song for me. Ongwynn had Morgause help her carry in extra water, and she heated the largest kettle over the fire, then called me to come bathe. She and Morgause had bathed in the cold spring pool, but there was warm water for me, to comfort every part of me including my soul, and Ongwynn washed my hair for me, and Morgause stood by and wrapped me in shawls when I was finished and made me sit by the hearth to stay warm.

Nurse, Ongwynn I mean, started gently combing the tangles out of my wet hair.

I felt blessed and grateful, and such warmth of heart is rare in me. I blurted, "Nurse, how did you come to us?"

She gave me her slow smile but said nothing.

"Because you are Ongwynn, I mean." Now I wanted my way, I wanted to know. "You are a wise woman, a white witch—"

She said, "You have more of the old, uncanny power than I ever will."

The memory of that power made me shiver. Still, I had saved Ongwynn. . . . I asked humbly, "It's not just the milpreve, then?"

"No! The milpreve came to you as a . . ." Ongwynn paused at length, listening within herself for the right word. "A sign," she said finally, "and a blessing, like the crown on a king."

"It knew me?" I had always felt this to be true.

"It knew you and chose you."

"Yet . . ." This was confusing. "Yet I needed it. . . ." The power had come to me through the milpreve. I sensed this surely.

Ongwynn said to me in her quiet way, "Yes, you must wear it. Without it you are still Morgan, but . . . is an uncrowned king still a king?"

I sat wondering yet delighted, for a king held his throne merely by birth and force, whereas I . . . I was chosen.

I had forgotten my question to Ongwynn, but Morgause had not. "Ongwynn, Morgan's right. If this is your home, what were you doing in Tintagel, being a servant?"

Ongwynn sighed in a way that meant she would answer

when she had formed the words; we knew this from long acquaintance with her silences. Morgause sat beside me on the hearthstone. We waited.

When she had combed every inch of my hair, Ongwynn said, "A sending told me to go."

"Sending?" I did not know what she meant.

"A dream. Strong. A vision in the night."

"Sent from whom?"

"Maybe the goddess mother of us all. Maybe fate. Maybe— I don't know. I am just a pedlar. I obey."

Morgause and I sat looking at each other, trying to puzzle this out.

Kneeling in front of me and to one side, Ongwynn started braiding my hair into many long plaits to make it ripple as it dried. "So I walked into Tintagel on the day of your birth, Morgan," she said.

As a child—that is to say, up until a few weeks before that day—I had assumed that Nurse had been there for me forever, like Tintagel, like the stones on which the castle stood. Morgause must have thought much the same, for she exclaimed, "I was a year old already?"

"Yes." This time Ongwynn's slow smile spread wide, almost mischievous. I had never seen such a smirk on her or such a glint in her pebble brown eyes. "You had another nurse taking care of you."

But then—but then why had they needed Ongwynn? I sat gawking.

She almost grinned. "I looked your mother and father in the eye," she said, "and told them I had come to nurse both of you girls, and that took care of it."

Green power.

The uncanny power of her gaze. The power she had used against armed guards to protect our escape from Tintagel. The power that had cost her so dearly that she had sickened and nearly died. I hesitated to speak of it, but I asked anyway, "It didn't tax you to do that?"

She knew exactly what I meant. Slowly she shook her head. "I was younger and stronger then."

I wondered whether there was not more to the matter than that, and I might have asked, but at that moment Thomas called from outside the portal, "May I come in yet?"

"Just a minute!" Morgause and I both shouted at once, and I bolted into my bedchamber, where a clean frock was laid out for me. It seemed that there had been a mighty washing of clothing during the day I lay abed, whether by my human companions or my small unseen ones I was not sure, but my sense was that the denizens helped those who were trying to do for themselves, and that Ongwynn and Morgause and Thomas had done much. The stone walls and ledges shone now from scrubbing. Sweet rushes lined the floors. Fat perch that Thomas had fished out of the spring pool lay cleaned and scaled and ready to poach for supper.

Dressed, I trotted back to the warmth of the hearth, where Ongwynn knelt at my other side and set to braiding my hair again. "Come in," she called to Thomas.

He did so, lugging a bundle of sticks and a sack of peat, which he unloaded, stacking the squares to dry near the fireplace. At first I listened only to the good feeling of Nurse's fingers tidying my head, but then the silence of Thomas's back began to work upon me, and I turned to look at him. He felt my look and gave me a half smile over his shoulder, but still he did not speak.

"What is wrong?" I asked him.

"Nothing."

Ongwynn let off plaiting my hair and turned to peer at him. He set the last square of peat in place, stood, straightened his shoulders and spoke to her.

"If all is well here," he said quietly, as if speaking of a bucket to be mended or a hare to be skinned, "I'll be leaving."

The words went through me like a spear. I leapt to my feet. "Thomas, no!" I cried before I realized it was not my place to speak.

Morgause spoke out of turn also. "Leaving? But Thomas, what for?"

He kept his eyes on Ongwynn's face, and to this day I am not sure whether he was speaking to her or to us. "It is not fitting that I should remain here."

And already in my heart of hearts I knew well enough what he meant. I had not yet experienced the monthly courses of a woman, and my breasts were just beginning to bud, but I felt the ache in me and I hoped he felt it too. I knew.

"No," I bleated like a child. "Thomas, no, stay, you must stay here with us!"

"Hush, Morgan." Lumbering to her feet, Nurse laid her palm upon my dewy, half-plaited head. "Thomas is right." To him she said, "Where will you go?"

He shrugged, and gave no other answer.

"Have you no home?"

He shook his head. "Like the youngest son of the poor nobleman in the old tale," he said, trying to joke, "I must venture forth to seek my fate."

"Fortune," Ongwynn corrected him, and leaving my hair half-dried and half-dressed as it was, she set about packing him a bag of provisions as if the word *fate* meant nothing to her. But it froze me into such a misery of fear for him that I could barely move, for I remembered: The midwife who had birthed Thomas, who might have been such a wise woman as Ongwynn herself, had said he was fated to die . . . I could not bear to think *in battle*, to remember the blind head on a pike like a scarecrow over death's ghastly garden, so I went numb. I sat on the hearth, hugging myself and watching the others as if watching reflections in water, hearing them as if they were very far away, without much comprehension.

"Give me no more than I can carry," Thomas was telling Ongwynn. "I'll leave Annie with you."

He was giving away his most precious companion. He saw death before him. I knew it. And—what could I do? Could I change his fate with the milpreve? To heal Ongwynn, I had somewhat promised to submit to my fate; was Thomas's fate part of mine? I did not know, I did not understand enough, I was not strong enough; I could do nothing. I could not move even to cry.

"Thomas, no," Morgause protested. "You don't have to leave Annie, you need her! How will you—"

"I'll walk."

"But—"

"I'm not trying to be noble," he said with a hint of exasperation. "I've outgrown her, that's all."

"But you'll miss her!"

I wished she had not said that. It made him wince.

I do not remember whether he replied, or how. Time became a sharp stone that skipped, rippling the watery images before my eyes. Thomas was saying his good-byes. Ongwynn reached up—Thomas was that tall now—and took his head in both her hands, blessing him.

"Protector, thank you for everything," he told her.

"You will meet with dangers," she said as levelly as if speaking of the weather.

"I know. I will be wary." He turned and hugged Morgause, then walked over to where I was sitting and—

I don't know what I was expecting or hoping for. A kiss? A pledge, a token?

He reached down and tugged one of my braids as if I were a child.

My chill misery heated in a flash. Fit to breathe fire, I leaped to my feet, yelling at him, "Stop it! Let me alone! Go on, get yourself killed, see if I care!"

His taut face flowered into a grin, and his eyes shone happy, like blue violets in the spring. "I'll be back," he said as if it were a taunt to provoke me. But then his voice gentled. "I'll be back, Morgan."

He whistled a lilting melody as he headed out the portal.

Three years passed without a word of him.

Three brief misty summers, three freezing winters, and every single day of those three years I brushed Annie and combed her mane and tail and cleaned her pretty face with a soft cloth and talked to her as if she were my best friend as I plaited her forelock between her sweet eyes. Year by year Annie's mane grew more silver, like Ongwynn's hair, her dapplings a lighter, brighter, more shining gray, her dark eyes more patient and wise. When I rode her to the distant village to barter fish or salt for the few things we needed—bolts of ticking for pallets, skeins of thread, spice for pickling, bodkins, fishhooks—when I rode her where folk might see her, I braided locks of her mane and tail as well, and bound them with red thread. This was folly, to draw attention so, and even the more folly that I rode alone and astride, but I could not seem to help it; I felt as if I must adorn Annie for Thomas's sake and ride her proudly as he would have done. Even though I wore a plain brown woolen frock like any peasant girl and hid my hair under a muslin cap, folk stared at me whenever I passed.

But in truth, any stranger would have been noticed in those lonely parts. "Who be ye, lass?" asked the goodwife from whom I bartered a setting of chicks.

I told her a name not my own. Meg or Peg, a commoner name; it doesn't matter what.

"Where be ye from?" These folk spoke an outlandish dialect; I could barely understand them.

"Ongwynn's hill."

She startled like a deer and flinched away from me. "Are ye a witch?" she gasped.

"No."

"Has—has the healer returned?"

"No." This was what Ongwynn had told me to say.

After word got around, I sometimes saw folk furtively cross themselves to ward off evil eye in my presence. Few spoke with me a word more than they had to. None of them came near Caer Ongwynn. This was as Ongwynn wished it.

Other than a few times a year when I rode Annie on such errands, I saw no one, spoke to no one except my sister and Ongwynn. I lived as if in a holy cell. And I say this not with regret, but with gratitude. In those years I learned knowledges forbidden to other women. Even my queen mother Igraine could not have learned such mysteries as I did.

The knowledges lived in the wooden chests stacked in the innermost chamber, the trunks Morgause and I had tried to open and could not. The day after Thomas left, Ongwynn led us into that chamber and opened the domed top of the uppermost chest with a touch.

"How did you do that?" I demanded.

Ongwynn gave her slow smile but did not answer.

"There's a spell on them," Morgause said. "There must be. See how they didn't rot like the wooden buckets and such."

Astonishment fraught me; Morgause had a brain? Morgause had thought of something that had not occurred to me? The realization shocked and mortified me silent as Ongwynn lifted from the chest its treasure.

Books.

Volumes great and small bound in tooled leather red or brown or black, sometimes inlaid with gold. I had seen books a few times before, in my father's chamber when he was alive and in Lord Steward Redburke's possession since, but never such elegant books, so many books—and in the possession of a woman? A common Cornishwoman? Books were not for commoners or women; everyone knew that. Yet there they were, in Ongwynn's hands, and she passed them to us as if they were meat pasties she was taking out of the oven. "Put them on the table."

We did, and ran back to find her bringing forth inks and vellums and quills such as scribes used. And when we had placed those on the table and returned, we found her lifting from the next chest rolled parchments limned with charts. And each trunk after that contained more wonders, wonders upon wonders that I could not yet begin to understand: circles within circles of gold orbs on gold wires, and vessels made of crystal, and a square block of polished wood inlaid with black tiles and white, and many figures carved from black walnut and pale ash wood. I gasped over these and took them one by one in my hands and saw nothing else for a while except a miniature carved white knight on a rearing charger, a black knight brandishing his sword, a grave bearded king under a heavy crown, a queen—oh, but the white queen was beautiful and sad and so much like my mother Igraine.

Always I tried not to think of my mother or wonder where she might be.

"What are the beads for?" Morgause asked behind me.

"To do sums upon."

My head snapped up, for an excitement I could not yet name jarred my spine. With the sad white queen still in my hand I spun to face Ongwynn. "For *who* to do sums?"

Some lord's steward, some king's seneschal, might do sums; why was I asking such a simpleminded question? Ongwynn would think I was stupid. She would say—

She said, "Me. You."

My jaw dropped so far I felt it click. I think Morgause could not speak either, for she did not.

"Come," said Ongwynn, and she led us to the table, where the books and inks and quill pens and vellums lay. She gestured for us to sit on the bench, and before each of us she placed a scrap of parchment and a pen. "We'll start with letters," she said.

Morgause gasped, "You're *lettered?*"

"Yes."

We gawked at her like simpletons.

"And so shall you be," she said.

The excitement bubbled and seethed within me like broth in the pot. To be lettered, like a scribe or a druid or a nobleman—it was an enormity, yet there was no denying that I desired—no, I yearned, I lusted for this learning as I had never lusted for the learning of loom or spinning wheel or embroidery. Thread and cloth were ordinary—worse than ordinary; they were women's affairs. But letters! Letters were for lords and kings. And something in me blazed fiery jealous and joyous at the thought: Why ever should they have what I did not?

"But you must keep the secret," Ongwynn added, "as I have."

We nodded. We knew that what we were doing was unheard-of—although in Caer Ongwynn it seemed possible; anything seemed possible there. Every night we left a food offering in the golden goblet that stood alone in the western chamber, a goblet fit for a king, and every morning the offering had been accepted, and every day unseen servants took care of half our needs. This was a place of powerful protection, and therefore a place where marvels could be ventured.

Only gradually did I come to understand that letters were a power and a magic just as surely as my milpreve was a tool of fearsome power. No wonder kings and lords denied letters to commoners and women.

Ongwynn showed us how to use our pens and started us practicing *Morgan* and *Morgause,* then sat and chose a book—small, bound in red leather tooled and illuminated with gold—and she opened it and began to read aloud.

> *Three women ride the white mare of the moon:*
> *Rhiannon with her silver bow hunting,*
> *Epona milkbreast suckling the king,*
> *Menwy the ancient hunchbacked crone,*
> *And these three be one.*

Because there was no need for her to find the words and pull them out of herself, because the book, or the unknown scribe who made the book, spoke through her, she spoke on steadily, strongly. She was no longer Nurse when she read aloud to us. She was no longer even Ongwynn. She became—something more. A druid, as she read to us the words of the druids:

> *Three mysteries are grasped by no man:*
> *The mistletoe green between earth and sky,*
> *The sadness in a maiden's smile,*
> *The runes shaped by the changing moon.*

7

"O NGWYNN," I DEMANDED, "TEACH ME POWER."

Sitting as stolid as a mountain across the table from me, she did not answer or even look at me, for she was contemplating her next move. Her stubby hand rested on the carved white queen whose sad, symmetrical face always made me think of my mother, which always made me try to think of other things.

In a clear, lilting voice Morgause read to Ongwynn and me as we played chess: *"But to the old queen, no mortal princess was beautiful enough for her son the prince, the king who would be. In every damsel with whom he danced she saw some flaw, whether hair less glorious than the sun or eyes less shining than the stars or bearing less graceful than that of a swallow on the wind. Dis . . .* Ongwynn, what is this word?"

Ongwynn gave her a quiet look.

"I know, I know." Morgause rolled her eyes and stared at the word, trying to puzzle it out. I jumped up and looked over her shoulder to see if I knew it. We were rivals at letters, Morgause and I, and therefore we learned quickly.

She got it first. *"Discontentment. Discontentment for her son's sake harrowed her—"*

I stuck out my tongue at her as I sat down. She whacked at me with the book and missed. Ignoring us, Ongwynn sat studying the chessboard. She still had not made her move. There was no hurry—not that Ongwynn ever hurried. But in wintertime particularly there was no hurry. During the short summers we were outdoors dawn to dusk with the chickens, the garden, picking wild strawberries and currants, scraping salt from the seaside rocks, gathering mussels, netting fish and drying them—but now the sleet pattered against the sealskin hung over the portal, snow and ice blanketed Ongwynn's hollow hill, and none of us were going anywhere for a while except to check on Annie in her snug little stable under the cliff, feed her dried seaweed and carrots, and bring in more firewood.

". . . she determined to give to her son a bride befitting him. She called her servants and ex . . . ex . . . exhorted them and sent them forth to bring to her every sweet blossom they could find, columbine and woodbine and wild rose and gillyflower, every blooming flower within twenty leagues. Messengers ran their horses to death to bring the queen the daintiest of woodland violets before the dew had dried from their petals. Then, surrounded by masses of flowers, the old queen shut herself in her tower chamber for seven days. And for every hour of those days thunder roared and lightning crackled around the tower—"

Ongwynn moved the white queen and said, "Check."

Blast. Such was the power of the queen, to strike from afar, while the king barely moved and had to be protected at all times. Yet my mother . . .

Morgause was reading, "*. . . at the end of the seven days the prince entered the queen's chamber to find his mother lying abed, smiling upon him as she died. And kneeling beside her, holding her frail hand, there gazed up at him a damsel more beautiful than any he had ever seen or could ever imagine, a damsel with skin like the most tender petals of the wild rose, eyes the color of violets shining with dew . . .*"

I castled my king to get him out of check. Stupid, timid king. Queen, knights, druids, men-at-arms all devoted to protecting him and fighting his battles—for what purpose?

"The prince fell in love with her at first sight."

The wind and icy rain seethed against the doorflap, the chickens huddled and drowsed in their mess of straw just inside the door, from somewhere behind my back I heard the whisperings and gigglings of the denizens, the piskies who might mend the hole in my stocking while I slept, or then again they might not, and I knew better than to turn and look; it would be wasted effort, and they would laugh aloud, for I would never see them.

This was my third winter at Caer Ongwynn and much the same as the first two. Morgause read in her tuneful voice, and later maybe we would sing a ballad or two just to defy the howling of the wind, and meanwhile I dreamed of warm, green, heather, larkspur, the earth a flower woman—yet I knew that spring would bring war again. Every time I rode Annie to the village I heard of battles, death, war and rumor of war. Winter was long, but at least it brought peace.

I wondered where Thomas was. How he fared. Whether he lived.

Morgause read, " 'Her name is Blossom,' said the queen. 'She is yours. She will do anything you desire, but she cannot speak. That you must never ask of her. I love you, my son.' Then the queen died, for she had given over her vital power to the damsel made of flowers."

I said to Ongwynn again, "Teach me power." I did not know how I would use it, but it would not be to make a damsel out of flowers.

Ongwynn glanced up from the board and gave me a flat look. "I am."

"This? A game of chess?" I lifted the queen carved of black walnut, her face as lovely as the white queen's but more grim. "Am I to hide a king behind my skirts someday? Did my mother—" But I had not meant to speak of my mother. I faltered into silence.

Ongwynn regarded me steadily now, her silence meshing with mine. Morgause stopped reading to listen.

After she had thought of the words, Ongwynn said, "Your mother loved your father."

Yes. Yes, my mother and father had loved with steadfast love, true love, as I loved Thomas. . . . The thought caught me by surprise, flowering out of me before I could stop it. It both warmed and frightened me.

"Such love softens a woman," Ongwynn said.

But—but I could not give up love . . .

Morgause put in, "Mother had power enough to protect us. Not power enough to keep Arthur, but—we don't know what happened after. Maybe things changed. We don't know. Maybe she had more power than we knew."

Ongwynn nodded and lifted one blocky hand to move her knight. "Checkmate."

Confound her. I studied the board. It was checkmate truly enough, and I did not see how she had done it to me.

"As usual," I grumbled. I swept my black chess pieces aside, reached for the white queen and cradled her in my hands. It didn't matter now what power the queen had. The game was over when the king went down.

Morgause laid her book aside. "Ongwynn, what are we to do with these—these powers you are teaching us? What do you foresee for us?"

Outside, not so far away, wind and sleet hissed like a serpent. Instead of answering, Ongwynn heaved herself up from the table and bent stiffly to feed more peat to the fire. Did her back hurt her? She had never said so. When had she started moving like an old woman?

"You don't have to do that," I complained as if her stiffness reproached me. "I can do that."

"There's little enough I can do." She straightened and faced Morgause. "I do not foresee," she said. "I am not a seeress."

"But you must have some idea."

"Thoughts, that is all."

"And?" Morgause prompted.

Ongwynn sighed out one of her long pauses before she spoke. "You are fated by birth to lives full of trouble," she said finally. "You are your mother's daughters."

Yes. Two half-grown girls hiding in Caer Ongwynn while

too many greedy men battled for an empty throne, and my mother the queen, wherever she was, had become no queen but only a pawn.

In a low voice Ongwynn said, "I think both of you will need to live by your wits. Be secret and strong."

"That's what I mean!" I burst out. "Teach me . . ." My hand hovered over my chest.

Ongwynn said softly, "Of that I know nothing."

"But—"

"I am a pedlar, that is all. Not a fay or a sorceress."

"Then teach me the power of a pedlar!"

"I can't."

Something as bleak as the weather in her tone made me catch my breath and blink. I had never before heard that shadow in her voice. Fays live on, Thomas had said, but pedlars . . . pedlars dwindle and die. The stark, dark undertone in Ongwynn's words made me hush and say no more.

Until that night, I had thought that it was to hide Morgause and me from prying folk that Ongwynn healed no colicky babies, eased no childbirth pangs. I had thought that she did not want the villagers coming to Caer Ongwynn. And perhaps it was so.

But perhaps . . . perhaps her power was weakening as she aged?

Or she had spent it all on us? Given us everything she had?

She sat down and said to Morgause, "Finish the story, child."

It was a simple enough story, and a sad one. The prince loved his blossom bride so desperately that he began to wonder, even though it should not have mattered to him, her husband and lord and master: Did she love him too? And even though it was a good thing for a woman to be silent, and even though Blossom complied with everything he required of her and fulfilled his every desire, he wanted her to say that she loved him in her heart. He came to yearn for this so wretchedly that he could not eat, he could not sleep, and at length his longing got the better of him. He asked her to bespeak to him her love. And she said yes, yes, my darling, I do love you, I love you utterly. But because he had violated the stricture that held the magic together, Blossom fell to pieces in his arms. Nothing but a few dry, dead petal fragments remained. The prince went sweetly mad. Even though his beloved flower bride had withered to dust in his arms, he thought that he could get her back somehow, somewhere. He spent his life wandering, searching for her and grieving for her until he died.

Even before my sending I grew restless. By my fifteenth summer, I had finally learned enough to defeat Ongwynn at chess, I knew the mysteries of adding sums upon beads, I understood how the planets and stars and sun and moon circled the earth on their invisible golden wires, I had read every book in Caer Ongwynn and some of them I had also heard read to me, and I knew by heart many of the stanzas of the book of threes:

> *Threefold is the love of a woman for a man:*
> *The crescent silver love of the maiden,*
> *The milk-white love of the mother of his child,*
> *The laughter of the crone in the dark of the moon.*

I knew the threes, and I thought I understood some of them. I was, of course, mistaken.

But I felt that I had learned all that Ongwynn could teach me and that I should be doing something—although I did not know what. Find Thomas? But how? Did he think of me as often as I thought of him? Did he love me? If I was his true love, I was to wait until he returned to me; all the stories of noble love said so.

Waiting was hard. I wanted to make something happen. It was a hard thing to be a woman.

When the wild strawberries were in bloom I started taking long rides on Annie for no reason. I rode on the moor, saw the blue violets with their heart-shaped leaves and thought of Thomas. I rode along the harsh stony beach at low tide and thought of Ongwynn. I rode through the silky white lace of breaking waves and thought of my mother. Igraine. Where was she now?

Where were my father's bones, so that I could lay a flower upon them?

Did my mother lie dead somewhere as well?

Ongwynn was—had lost her powers, it seemed, and was stiffening in her joints, was getting old. The thought that she would someday die chilled my spine. I had never quite been able to think of her as just a person. Had she been born? I could not imagine Ongwynn with a mother and a father, I could not conceive that she had ever been a child. Even less imaginable, had she ever known the love of a man? Had she ever borne a child?

How long had she lived?

I could not ask her. It was not that I was afraid of Ongwynn, but—she was all humble dignity; I would have buried my head in mud before I ventured such questions to her.

Growing old, would she need me? I ought to stay with her.

I wanted to leave.

"Ongwynn," I asked her as we sat in the sun and mended hose (for the piskies had given me hair ribbons so gossamer they seemed made of moonlight, but had not darned my stockings), "Ongwynn, I wish—I don't know what I wish. What can I do?"

She glanced up at me without speaking, her eyes like stones washed round by the sea.

I said, "How can I give it back to you?"

"Give me what?"

"What you've lost."

"I've lost nothing."

"What I owe, then."

"You owe nothing."

"But—"

"When you are older you will see," she said, and she went back to her darning with a decided silence. I could say no more.

The sending began as nothing more than a dream.

I lay deeply asleep after a day of weeding and spading in the garden. And as with most dreams, I cannot remember it clearly, only shards and shadows. There was something about Annie, sweet round dapple-gray Annie, cantering up the night sky, leaping over the starry Indy blue darkness into the clouds, but then she was the round dappled moon as full as a new mother's breast and as white and—rose, the moon was a rose and the

89

moon rose, growing so that it filled my sight, growing, blossoming. It was the moon yet it was flowers, many flowers white and damask and apple dapple harvest gold and true violet blue, it was moonflowers yet it was a blossom woman smiling at me through clouds of gossamer hair ribbon, smiling and calling me by name: Morgan.

And it was she, the gay, green-eyed, half-naked fay garlanded with primroses, laughing and speaking to me just as she had that day in Caer Avalon: "Morgan. Do you know why you are here?" It was she, that maiden innocent of shame—yet it was an ancient gray crone, as hunchbacked as the waning moon, cackling.

And it was a black vulture circling with a craking cry.

And it was the moon.

And it was Mother.

Igraine. Her lovely face as hollow and gray as a skull.

And it was a voice as big as the moonlit night calling me: Morgan. Morgan! Come here.

I awoke sobbing, but it was not just a dream. The faces remained before me in the darkness of my chamber, shimmering like the moons and stars on Merlin's midnight velvet cloak, but—but I did not understand, the faces were many yet one, a ghostly changing crescent-full-decrescent moon made of flower women hovering close to my face, and their voices—their many voices were one voice, honey sweet but as great as sky, saying, "Morgan, come to Avalon. Come to Avalon, daughter."

The face of many faces faded away into the darkness, and the voice whispered away yet echoed like a shout within my mind. I jumped up from my bed, weeping like a child, as hard as I had wept the day they cooked my favorite frock black, and

I ran barefoot through the cold, stony darkness to Ongwynn's chamber. It must have been the dead of night, with not even mice or piskies rustling, although somewhere an owl spoke. I folded to my knees by Ongwynn's pallet and shook her shoulder, but she was already awake, already struggling to sit up and see what was the matter with me.

"I'm sent for," I cried.

Ongwynn sat on her pallet, and I could feel more than see her quiet gaze upon me. Morgause pattered in, roused by my noise, saying, "Morgan, what in the world—"

"Her," I blurted between sobs, "the—the flower fay—and— all, they all said—come to Avalon—"

"A sending?" Ongwynn asked, her voice as level as ever in my life.

I could barely speak. "Ye—yes."

She lifted her common, heavy hands and placed one on each side of my head just as she had for Thomas, like a blessing. And there was something of the healer left in her after all, for her touch calmed my tears and my heart.

"Then go, Morgan," she said.

No. No, I couldn't. I had to stay with Ongwynn. I had to wait for Thomas to come back to me.

"Go," Ongwynn said again, soft as dawn.

It was my fate calling, I sensed. And healing Ongwynn, I had promised to obey my fate. I knew I had to go.

More: I knew I wanted to.

BOOK THREE
Avalon

8

I LEFT AT DAWN, ON ANNIE. SHORT OF BEING KNOCKED
on the head I could not possibly have gone back to sleep that
night, and no one else did either. Ongwynn got up, got dressed,
and set about provisioning me. I dithered back to my chamber
with a rushlight in hand and tried to get some clothing onto
myself and some into a bag; I kept changing my mind about
which should go where. Morgause drifted around my chamber
like a spirit, great-eyed and silent and annoying. "I can't think
with you hovering," I complained. "Go back to bed."

She did not, but she ghosted out after a while, then slipped
back into my chamber and said, "Here," holding something
small toward me.

"What?"

She said nothing. I had to take it to see what it was: a ring
woven of human hair. Mother's hair.

"I don't need that." I tried to hand it back to her.

"Take it with you," Morgause told me.

"Why? I'll be back."

Morgause just gave me the look of a big-eyed deer mouse caught in candlelight.

"Oh, for the love of mercy . . ." I put the ring on a finger of my right hand and turned my back, going about my packing.

The piskies didn't care that Morgause was silently saying I might be killed. They chuckled and chittered and rustled everywhere in my chamber, so excited that several times I almost caught sight of them, glimpsing movement from the corner of my eye, shadows scampering. And whenever I lacked for anything, I had only to turn my back and when I turned around again, it would magically be there. When my rushlight burned out, a candle flame without a candle lit my chamber. When I needed string for bundling, silken cord appeared. When I realized I had only a few shabby patched frocks and a crude homemade pair of shoes by way of clothing, I turned around to find fine soft leather boots and a full dozen gowns—not the frocks of a girl or the skirts of a peasant woman, but the flowing silk-and-velvet garb of a lady. I stood there with my mouth open as the piskies laughed at me, the sly little never-seen brats, and to this day I do not know whether the gowns were magicked in a moment or took months in the making, whether they somehow knew beforehand that I would have need of a lady's clothing.

"Thank you, brats," I managed to say at last, and they laughed at me more than ever.

Morgause stood gazing at the gowns as if they had dropped onto my bed out of the moon.

"Here," I told her, "I don't need all these. You take some of them." We were the same size, she and I, and we still looked almost as much alike as twins, Ongwynn said, but I was the one who could be counted upon to be making noise or difficulty. "Which would you like? The rose-colored ones?" She could have those. I hated pink.

She shook her head. "They're yours."

"I want to give you some! Which ones?" I grabbed a satin gown that looked like a frothy sea at sunset, and tried to hand it to her, but all by itself it flew out of my arms and landed on my bed again.

"They're yours," Morgause said.

"But Annie can't carry all this!" I wailed.

Such silliness, fretting over satin and lace when I was setting forth to make my way alone through wilderness or battlefields or both.

In the end, I wore the fine new boots to ride in, put on a blue velvet gown with my oldest frock over it to protect it, decided I would need a straw bonnet to keep the sun out of my eyes and jammed it on my head so I wouldn't forget it, brushed Annie by moonlight and braided her mane with gossamer hair ribbons, and I am sure I looked like a madwoman. I packed what I could and left the rest behind. At first dayspring light I saddled Annie and hooked my bags behind the cantle. In one of them, Ongwynn had packed one of her precious parchment charts, though I protested that I did not need it; Morgause and I had studied those charts. I knew the ways of the rivers, the mountains, and the warring lords between me and Avalon.

I hugged and kissed Morgause, hugged Ongwynn—I think it was the first time I had ever hugged Ongwynn. I had hugged Morgause sometimes in play or mischief, just as I had sometimes pinched her or yanked her hair, but I had seldom touched Ongwynn except that one time when I healed her. Hugging her was like hugging a warm mountain as solid as bedrock. I kissed her timidly on her cheek. It was heathery dry.

It was not until I had mounted Annie that the enormity of what was happening gripped my heart. Till then I had dithered from chamber to chamber and task to task, but now there stood Ongwynn and Morgause like doorposts outside the portal of Caer Ongwynn, and the air hung thick with rainbow mist, and for some reason I noticed the roaring of the sea as I looked at my sister and Ongwynn, my rock, and already they seemed far, far away. Whether I would ever see them again only the goddess—or whatever fey force had taken charge of my life—only the moon knew.

"You're a sight," Morgause said, trying to make me smile, but I couldn't.

"Do you have your stone?" Ongwynn asked, and for a moment I heard in her voice an echo of Nurse—my nurse of so far ago and long away. I felt tears trying to sting their way out of my eyes. I wouldn't let them.

"Of *course* I have my stone," I grumbled, lifting my hand to make sure even though I could feel it nestling warm between my half-grown breasts—at least I hoped they were only half grown, for they did not amount to much.

Morgause said, "Come back safely," and although I am sure she tried to keep her voice as level as Ongwynn's, it wavered.

Come back. And the thought that I had been trying not to think burst from me. I blurted, "If Thomas comes back while I am gone . . ."

"I'll marry him," Morgause said, trying to tease.

I could have breathed fire at the thought. I scorned her, for a moment I hated her, and the moment freed me to go. "Good-bye," I whispered, and I raised my hand to wave farewell as I sent Annie cantering away.

On that journey I discovered that Annie, also, was mine only to lose, like everything else I had ever counted on.

That was very long ago, and now I fly with the cloud shadows, and one would think I could stop caring. But looking back, I still hate myself for my stupidity. For three years Annie had been ridden seldom and had been feeding on thistles and scant grass, yet I thought only of myself—I expected her to be a swift messenger pony again and carry me like the wind to Avalon. And it pains me still when I remember how loyally she tried to do so.

The first few days on the springy turf of the upland moors I galloped her until her ribs heaved and sweat foamed on her neck. And I thought all was well. I could see unto the horizon in every direction nothing more dangerous than sheep, and the honeybees suckled at the heather under a vast blue sky, and I felt like a half-fledged young hawk just out of the nest; I wanted to fly.

I saw no reason to be secret so long as I told no one my true name. It had been three years; I hoped Redburke and others who might want me dead had forgotten about me. Also, if there was fighting between me and Avalon, I wanted to know about it. When I met with cowherds or tinkers or the like, I gave them greeting and asked them, "What news?" Or if there was a village, I would ride in and drink water at the common well and give water to Annie when she had cooled enough so that it would not harm her, and I would ask of folk who stopped to stare what was the name of the place, to guide my course by. Almost always folk stammered when they replied as if they were trying to decide whether they needed to tug their forelocks and bow to me. Some folk were wary, some curious, some friendly. A goodwife gave me scones to eat, a goatherd gave me cheese, and I bartered Annie's ribbons for oats for her. Few folk were bold enough to ask whence I came or where I was going, and in answer to the bold few I only smiled and rode on. And three times in as many days I changed my course because of the cautions they gave me. In the distance sometimes I could see the dust of battle rising like the smoke, as if the earth herself were burning, and I shuddered.

During the nights Annie either grazed or lay down, and I slept under the stars sometimes, in a sheepcote sometimes and once in a cowshed on the outskirts of a village when it was raining. I slept lightly, for I missed the murmur of the sea, and these soft inland hills felt strange to me, too tame with their maple groves, their villages huddled in hollows, their hedged garden plots. Also, the summons of Avalon tugged at me like a golden wire threaded into my heart, and I wanted only to ride on.

I cantered across the cushiony hills, and my heart sang like a harp of Avalon, Avalon, and I felt blessed, exalted.

I thought nothing could harm me.

Then I reached the mountains.

I saw them rising in the distance out of wilderness that coiled like an ivy green shadow around their feet, and I felt my mouth open like a hollow moon. Now I am ancient or ageless and I have flown over snowpeaks and I know what mountains are, but then I was a maiden like a green willow sprout, only fifteen, and those crags were the most daunting tors I had ever seen.

Within a day's journey the land changed from heathery moor to rocky foothills, and Annie went lame.

At first when I felt the hitch in her gait I thought that she had a stone wedged in her hoof, and I jumped down from her back and lifted her feet one by one. No stone. But one of her little clay-colored hooves, the left fore, had begun to crack.

"Oh, Annie . . ." I stood there harrowed by the knowledge that I was selfish, thoughtless, stupid. I should have had metal plates put on her hooves the way the knights did before they set out on a long journey. It was not often done for farm ponies and such, but probably in some village I could have traded something, maybe one of those confounded gowns, to have a blacksmith do it. But now the villages lay behind me, and the dust of war rose on that horizon, and it was too late. A mystic force tugged at me the way the moon tugged at the tides, pulling me toward Avalon, Avalon, Avalon.

Perhaps I could have pitted the force of my stubborn self-will against that sending, if only for a day, and turned back to see Annie safely pastured. But I did not. I wanted to go on.

I straightened Annie's forelock between her eyes, for all the good that did. "Sweetheart," I whispered to her, "I'm so sorry."

I got on her again and rode at the walk, seeking the softest ground. The rocky uplands gave way to copses of willow and rowan, and I rode a twisting course over the loam and leaves beneath the trees, hoping Annie's hoof would get no worse.

But it did. By evening the hoof had begun to split.

By evening also, copses of maple had given way to such wilderness as I had never seen. Huge trees—their ivy-shrouded trunks of greater girth than Annie and I put together, towering so high I could not see the sky—tree giants whose names I did not know shadowed me all around, and the darkness at night in that forest was like the darkness underground. By the last whisper of gray twilight I gazed up, seeking a glimpse of even a single star, and saw only a mesh of branches in which clustered—dark moons? Black posies with no stems? Balls of something that seemed to belong neither to earth nor sky.

"Annie," I murmured, "is that mistletoe?" It had to be. Then these were oak trees. And this was a druid wood.

I did not sleep much that night.

In the morning I saddled and bridled Annie and loaded my gear, then looked again at her hoof, bit my lip and started walking, holding the reins as she limped along behind me.

"Please let us pass," I said to the wilderness, for I felt as if it were alive, watching us, and not at all sure it liked us. The air felt thick and shadow gray, as if a cloud had caught and settled there, as if the sun never shone.

I needed to set a course mostly uphill in order to cross the mountains, but the way was blocked by rocks, tangling vines, fallen trees, some of them greater of girth than I was tall. The forest twisted and turned me so that I lost all sense of getting anywhere, and it was full of strange sounds; leaves rustled when there was no wind, trees groaned, and sometimes I seemed to hear something or someone laughing at me. Once I heard a scream that might have been human or not. I listened, listened, and learned nothing, and sweated with fear so that I could not slow down, stop, rest, let Annie rest. Every moment, some snicker or whisper in the forest spurred me on, and at the same time the song of Avalon buzzed in my bones, urging me onward until every muscle ached.

Some slopes were so steep that I needed to hang on to saplings to pull myself up. And I needed the use of my hands to drag deadwood aside or bend branches away, and between that and holding on to the reins to lead Annie, I tripped over my long skirt until, in exhaustion and a kind of muted fury, I sat down on the dirt, took my knife and hacked off a quantity of lovely blue velvet. I threw the cloth aside, but then for a wonder I had an intelligent thought, and I retrieved it and said, "Annie, give me your foot."

I suppose I was talking to keep myself from looking over my shoulder all the time, to pretend I was not all alone, but Annie just gave me that blank stare horses do so well. I stood up, looped the reins over her neck, lifted her foot and wound the cloth around and under her split hoof, then tied it in place as sturdily as I could. This solved nothing, I knew, but I hoped it would make her more comfortable. "Poor Annie," I told her, then I sighed and struggled on, and Annie hobbled behind me so closely that sometimes she nuzzled the back of my neck. It took me a while to realize that I had left the reins looped over her neck. She was following me on her own.

By evening, in my fine boots and fine hose, I was limping almost as badly as she. And I was still hearing the laughing voices in the forest. And it was raining. I did not sleep much that night either.

I have always been stubbornly slow to deal with anything that fails to take heed of my plans. When gray morning came I padded my blistered feet with kerchiefs inside the boots, and I replaced the wrapping on Annie's hoof with a new one just as thick, but I put the saddle and bridle on her again. Then we limped on as before, uphill through the shadows under towering trees whose names I did not know, winding our way between crags and deadfalls, tripping over roots and vines and fallen limbs and into hollows hidden under drifts of leaves even though it was the height of summer. I hated that forest by then, but feared it so much I did not dare to show my hatred. When for perhaps the fortieth time a branch knocked the straw bonnet off my head, I said, "Keep it," and walked on. Around midday something in my mind snapped to attention and saw both sense and hopelessness. I stopped, pulled the saddle off Annie and tossed it aside, and took off the bridle and did the same. After I had rigged the packs so that they would stay in place on her back, we went on.

Again, this solved nothing except that Annie limped on with a free head and a lighter load. But I smiled when I felt her warm breath stirring the hair over my ear.

Our luck changed then, or so it seemed. Sometime that afternoon we happened upon a path of sorts running up the mountain, and we followed it.

I did not have the sense to turn aside and hide in the forest when I heard the clatter of hooves approaching from in front of us.

I suppose he did not hear us, for he was making more noise than we were. And in that shadowland we came almost nose to nose before he saw us and stopped, staring.

I answered his stare and did not smile, for I did not like his looks. I have never liked it when men don't keep their beards and hair clean. He rode a fine horse, but he was no knight; he wore a dirty leather jerkin and no hat. Behind his horse trailed several others roped together. Only two carried his packs; the others wore headstalls and saddles with gear lashed to them, bridles and swords and spears and such.

"Well, greetings to you too," he said.

I didn't like his smile. It was yellow and oily. It was not until afterward that I realized he had every right to stare at me standing there with *my* hair none too clean either, escaping from its braids, and my old brown frock over my hacked-off velvet gown and Annie following me with no headstall, no lead rope, in her velvet footgear.

"Greetings," I mumbled. "What news?"

Instead of answering me he jerked his chin toward Annie. "That's a pretty pet you have there."

I did not answer.

"What is she? An Irish pony?"

I just looked at him, stupid with weariness.

"There's good breeding in her. What's wrong with her? Cracked hoof?" he asked.

"Yes."

"She just needs to rest, then. Trim it, let it grow out again, good as new."

I nodded, but this was cold comfort. There was no haven in this wilderness where I could stop and let Annie rest and not starve to death myself. Also, I had to go on. The call of Avalon would not let me do otherwise.

He must have seen something of the thought in my face, for he said, "You need a horse you can ride? I'll trade you."

I did not respond, so dull with weariness that the words made no sense to me.

"The dun, or the bay at the end there, or even the chestnut

gelding," he said. "They're strong, sound horses, carry you anywhere you want to go."

He wanted to barter me a horse in trade for Annie? It was barely thinkable, yet . . . I looked full at him for the first time and saw him eyeing Annie the way I had sometimes seen the menservants back in Tintagel eyeing the scullery maids.

He said, "I'll take her off your hands. I know a place not too far down country where they'll pasture her."

At the time I still thought that there were ways to make right decisions and wrong decisions, and I stood with my breath stuck like a lump of ice in my chest, trying to think what would be right. Avalon called to me, sang and sobbed and cried out in me, Avalon, Avalon, hurry, you're sent for, and I could have a strong horse to carry me quickly there, and Annie—maybe Annie would be better off not having to stumble along after me. . . .

"I'll even throw in an old bridle, and a blanket for you to ride on," the horse trader said.

I looked at Annie, and it wasn't just her beauty, or even the way my every memory of Thomas looked back at me out of her gentle dark eyes; it was—it was her faithfulness. I could not let her go. Avalon be cursed, I just couldn't do it.

I shook my head, bent my gaze to the stones of the trail and began to trudge on.

"I'll throw in a *saddle*," the horse trader cried.

"No. Annie stays with me."

For a few breaths there was a silence as Annie and I made our slow way past him and his mount. Then he shouted after me, "You're a fool, missy!"

Oddly, this made me smile. Looking back at him over my shoulder, almost laughing, I said, "I know it."

My smile must have touched him somehow, for he pressed his lips together, then grumbled, "Beware. The tor's infested with knights errant."

That made me lose my smile. It chilled my spine, and I turned around to look at him as if to ask him to please say he was joking. Knights errant knew only one rule: Might Meant Right. Later, Arthur and his jolly round table were able to change that somewhat—much later. But till then, knights without a lord meant only trouble.

The horse trader saw my shock and gave me his greasy grin. "Fighting like rats in a barrel. That's where I got this lot." He jerked his head at his string of horses. "Victor doesn't always get the spoils. Not if the victor's dead too."

"Oh." Half sick, I took a long breath. "I'll be careful. Thank you."

"You're still a fool," he snapped, and he rode on with his nags trailing behind him.

Annie nuzzled the back of my neck as I walked on, footsore, ever deeper into the wilderness of which I did not then know the name: the Forest Perilous.

9

THAT ROUGH, DIRTY, GREEDY RASCAL OF A HORSE trader was a gentleman compared to what lay ahead.

Thanks to his warning, when next I heard the rhythm of hooves on stone, I turned aside from the track. If I had not lamed Annie, damn my stupidity, she could have carried me swiftly into the forest and away—but as it was, we did not have much time. I grabbed Annie by the forelock and whispered to her, "Hurry!" But she had not hobbled much more than ten limping steps off the path when, with his chain mail jangling and the saddle leather creaking under his armored weight, the knight rode past. All I could do was freeze like a rabbit, staring, and hope the knight did not look my way.

Luck was with me. He rode with his visor down, so unless he turned his head he could see only straight before him. I noticed smears of brownish red on his shield and armor—at first I thought it was rust, but a moment later I knew better—then I had to choke back horror that would have made me cry out.

At his knee, hanging by its hair, swung the severed, dripping head of what had once been a man.

He rode past, and I leaned against Annie's solid warmth and took several deep breaths to keep from retching.

Then we went on. A small distance up the trail Annie shied; any horse will shy at the smell of fresh blood. Just off the path lay the beheaded body. I shuddered and passed by.

Later that same day I barely got Annie off the path before another knight passed by, this one with a squire riding behind him. The knight wore his visor, but it was just blind luck that the squire did not see us.

The next day luck turned against us.

That day for a wonder the sun shone golden through the green trees. The sunshine lifted my heart. But for years afterward I distrusted such green-gold days, as if they might mean a cruel trick of fate.

I remember how the sunlight gleamed on the black charger decked in scarlet as the knight rode up the path, as I watched him from between the trees with Annie by my side, as I kept silence, almost certain that he would pass by like the others. I remember how sun rays glistered on his hulking trunk draped in chain mail, his greaves, his gauntlets, his red-plumed helm, his visor behind which I could see only shadow. I remember how that golden light caught on his sword hilt and the device on his shield—a red griffin rampant. I remember how it glinted on the lance his squire carried—

I gasped. The squire was Thomas.

The knight heard my gasp and turned his head. "Oh ho," he said, wheeling his charger and spurring it toward me.

I scarcely heard him or saw him, for Thomas's wide-eyed

gaze met mine, and time had stopped for me. Thomas. His shoulders broader, his jaw harder, and a shadow in his sky blue eyes that was new to me, but still that steady regard. True Thomas.

The knight halted his steed beside me, reached down and seized me above the elbow with a grasp of steel.

Shock made me scream and struggle even before I realized what was happening. With all my small strength I strove to wrench myself free from his rough grip, glimpsing his wintery eyes through his visor. My thrashings only made him scowl. "Stupid wench," he growled, tightening his fingers. "Stop it. You're mine." Might meant right. Because he was stronger, he could take me and do what he would with me.

As if from another, kinder world I heard Thomas cry, "Annie!" and shout something I did not understand. Annie shrilled and reared, striking the knight full in his mailed chest with both forehooves.

She almost unseated him. Only the high cantle of his saddle kept him from toppling. He lost his grip on me, and let out a yell of anger. Off balance from pulling against him, I fell hard to the rocky ground, and there I lay with the breath knocked out of me, gawking up uselessly. I saw Thomas charging, riding low over his horse's neck with lance couched, spurring the steed between trees, trying to save me. I saw Annie rear again—

The knight drew his broadsword and lopped off Annie's head.

Just like that, like killing a rat. My Annie.

I saw the sword flash like a brown trout leaping, saw the spurt of vivid red—heart's blood, brighter than any flower that ever bloomed. Annie's blood. I saw her head fly, her eyes still living and terrified for a moment as she died.

At the same time Thomas drove into the knight with the lance. But the knight wheeled, and Thomas's blow slipped off his breastplate. The knight bellowed, "What! Traitor!" and his shield struck the lance aside. With his sword already reddened by Annie's blood he turned on Thomas.

No. Please, no. I lurched to my feet. Thomas had no armor, no weapon, not even a leather jerkin to protect him. He threw up his arm to block the first blow and gave a shout more like a scream: "Morgan, *run!*"

I stood by Annie's lifeless body. I saw blood, that reddest of all reds, well from Thomas's arm and shoulder. The sword lifted again.

I snatched the milpreve out from under my dress; it blazed like blue fire, so bright it blinded me, so hot it burned my hand, but not as hot as the fire dragon inside me roaring, raging, rearing to smite. I shrieked, "Death to that knight! Kill him! Kill—"

The power knocked me off my feet, slammed me against an oak and drove me to the ground. I did not get to see the knight fall dead.

I awoke a few moments later feeling as if his gauntleted fist had struck me down. Thomas crouched over me, clutching his wounded arm and panting with pain. Blood trickled between his fingers.

"Thomas!" Weak and dazed, I struggled to my knees beside him.

"You saved my life," he whispered.

"Who saved whom?" I ripped at the frock I wore over my dress and managed to yank it off. Easing his hand aside, I started to wrap the wound, trying to stop the flow of blood.

"Morgan," he murmured, and he leaned his head against my shoulder and fainted.

I piled on top of Annie's body anything that I could find to keep the carrion birds off her: branches, stones, the dead knight's shield and mail and armor. I wrested all his warrior gear off him and left him sprawled in his woolens; the crows and ravens could have him. Let them feast on him soon; it galled me to see not a mark on him. His dead eyes staring out of his grizzled beard looked surprised, that was all. I wanted to put my heel to his cruel nose and cave his face in for hurting Thomas and killing Annie, but I didn't do it; I knew the memory would sicken me later, and there was already enough to sicken me.

By the time I got Annie covered, I no longer noticed that I was crying. Sobs came out of me rhythmically, just a noise like the turning of a mill wheel. I kept an eye on Thomas lying wrapped in my mantle on a patch of moss under a gigantic tree. He had a deep cut in his shoulder and a long bloody gash in his arm. I had wrapped the wounds as tightly as I could and swaddled his arm against his body so that he would not move it, then laid him there. He had not stirred or moaned, and I hoped he was still unconscious of his pain, but as I finished building my makeshift cairn over Annie, he turned his head and whispered, "Morgan."

I trotted over to him and knelt beside him. He looked up at

me, his blue eyes narrow and clouded. His free hand wavered toward my face.

He murmured, "Don't cry."

Reminded that I was crying, I could barely hold back the sobs. Tears ran down my face.

Thomas whispered, "Is it—Ongwynn?"

"No." I rubbed my face dry with my blue velvet sleeve; it was filthy and I am sure so was I. "No, Ongwynn was well when I left."

"Morgause?"

"She's with Ongwynn."

"But why—why are you—"

"Hush." Later I would tell him why I was out here wandering the mountain, why I had gotten Annie killed, curse everything, curse Avalon and the sending that had brought me here, curse my idiocy that had made Annie lame, curse that foul knight—I felt fiercely glad that I had killed him. But at the same time the memory of my own power chilled me.

Could I kill people anytime I wanted now?

Could I plan for this? Or did rage make me do it?

Whom would I kill next?

I shivered and brushed the thoughts aside. There was no time for thinking right now. "We have to move," I told Thomas. "Get away from here." Away from the path and away from the bodies.

He nodded and struggled to sit up.

"Wait," I told him, "let me bring your horse first." I ran to where I had tethered the stolid bay nag and led it to him. He could not quite stand until I reached to help him; then he pulled himself to his feet, swaying. His blue gaze focused on my hand, still clutched in his. "You're hurt," he declared in round-eyed bewilderment, as if this could not be so. Holding my hand palm up, he stared at a raw hole seared into the flesh, a burn about the size of a walnut.

"It's nothing." I had barely noticed the mark, not even to wonder what had done it to me; my hurts were not worth bothering about compared to his.

He kept hold of my hand. "You have a sweetheart?"

"No. Why?"

"The—the ring."

The ring woven of soft sable brown hair. "My mother."

"Queen Igraine! I—I have been trying to find her. . . ." He let go of me and grabbed for the nearest tree to stay upright, closing his eyes against his own weakness.

"Thomas, no more talking." I snatched up my mantle from the ground. "We have to get you on this horse. Can you put your foot in the stirrup?"

He did, and grasped the mane with his free hand and tried to swing himself up, but could not make it. He slumped with his belly across the saddle.

"Stay there," I told him.

He mumbled something. ". . . try again."

"Thomas, *stay* the way you are." I chirruped at the horse and tugged the reins to get it moving.

I led it at a gentle walk—but there is no such thing as *gentle* when the way leads up a wilderness mountain. Thomas was moaning by the time we had gone half a furlong. But only a little farther, I found a rocky scarp to give us shelter of sorts and, for a wonder, a trickle of water. I stopped the horse and eased Thomas off it.

He folded to the ground and gasped. "Morgan, what are you doing here?"

"Plaguing you," I snapped, and I threw my mantle over him, then left him for a moment while I ran back for Annie's packs and the knight's black charger. I threw the bags over the black horse, trotted it back to Thomas, and pulled the gear off both horses, dumping their saddles and bridles and packs in a mess on the ground. Then like a badger I started rooting through the baggage. That accursed knight was well provisioned; at least we would not lack food while Thomas healed. Soup, I thought vaguely. Might there be a kettle in this muddle? Make fire, make soup. Find a soft place for Thomas, moss, leaves, bracken, find blankets, make a proper bed for him—

"Morgan," he murmured.

I left the packs and knelt beside him. It hurt me to look at him lying so pale, so beautiful, so perilously hurt. Blue shadows lay on his tender eyelids. He did not open his eyes.

"I'm right here," I told him.

"Did he hurt you?"

"No! I'm fine." Every part of me ached as if I had been thrashed, but my heart hurt worst. Annie. Thomas.

"Gypsy—pony," Thomas whispered.

"Yes."

"Mane like—lady's hair."

"Yes." Yes, I had kept Annie shining, even on the journey. My gentle Annie. I had never known it was in her to fight like that. To save me.

"Morgan, you—you grew."

He was lying there with his eyes closed, talking almost in his sleep, but I became suddenly, blushingly conscious of the way the velvet gown bared my neck and clung to my breasts.

"Hush," I told him, my voice not quite under control. "Go to sleep before I take a rock to you." I went off to tend campfire, make soup and all the rest of it. When I felt sure Thomas was deeply sleeping, I pulled off the ragged, filthy gown, washed myself at the icy trickle of springwater, and put on one of my old brown frocks.

"No," said Thomas.

"But I am sure I can do it."

"No. It'll hurt you."

We sat whispering like the trees in the night, leaning against the rocks and listening to the darkness, the forest breathing, the silences and screams and hootings and wild laughter of neither of us knew what. It was our third night in that wilderness, and Thomas felt strong enough now to sit up and keep watch with me for a while. But his face showed moon pale in the light of my milpreve. I held it on my lap, and it shone there like a blue star. I had put out the cooking fire for fear of attracting unwelcome company; the milpreve was our only light.

"It won't hurt me much," I said doubtfully. I wanted to use the milpreve to heal him. All day every day the summons of Avalon tugged like a fishhook in me, and all night every night; I paced in the dark and could not sleep. I had to travel. But I could not leave him.

"Not much?" he mocked gently. "Just burn a hole in you, blacken your eyes, knock you down—"

"I don't mind."

"Morgan—" He sat forward to face me, his tone stark serious. "That stone terrifies me. Put it away. Please."

I could not refuse him anything he asked of me in that way. I lifted the milpreve and let it drop inside my gown—some whim had made me wear the sea green gown, and I had plaited my hair in a crown and wound it with ivy just for something to do. I had put a garland of ivy on Thomas too, to amuse him. But neither of us could see the other in the dark. His voice came to me out of shadows.

"The milpreve," he said. "Is that the reason you must go to Avalon?"

"I don't know."

"You don't know who wants you there or why?"

I shook my head.

"Morgan?" He could not see me.

"I think it's the moon," I mumbled.

"That fits," he said. "Lunacy."

We had been through this. The first time I had mentioned the name of Avalon, it had shocked his breath away. It was a place where no one ventured, he had told me, not even warring lords, not even renegade knights. Or if knights ventured there, they came back mad and gibbering and unable to say what terror lay there, or they did not return at all.

"The moon," I said, "or the youngest fay, the primrose one."

I did not have to explain to him. He knew of these things, as Ongwynn had said the night he had guessed her name. The Gypsies had spoken of these things around their campfires. Some folk said that the language of the Gypsies was the language of fays and magic, the language that spoke to flowers and animals, a language that could tell a placid little dapple-gray pony to rear up and strike an armored knight.

"You're never likely to face a greater peril," whispered Thomas.

"I know," I said. Actually, I did not know. I did not understand then, or for years to come, how I carried my greatest peril to Avalon within my heart.

"Morgan, do you really have to go there?"

"Yes. The calling in me . . ." I could not begin to explain to him the yearning so strong it took away my fear and made me feel as if I should have been at Avalon yesterday. I murmured, "If only there were someplace safe for you to stay . . ." I let the thought trail away, for I knew of no safe place in the world except Caer Ongwynn, much too far away.

"No," said Thomas, "I will go with you."

10

I RODE THE DEAD KNIGHT'S BLACK HORSE, FOR I HAD the use of both arms and hands, and I needed them and the fierce curb bit and all my strength to control that steed; the big brute wanted to charge, not walk. My hands were blistered by the reins after the first day of struggling with him. Thomas rode the more placid bay, mounting from a tree stump and holding the reins with his one good hand. He sat erect, his injured arm in a sling, his face quiet and proud and much too pale. I knew that for his sake we should have stayed where we were another few days if not a fortnight. But he said he was ready to ride, and I could not help but take him at his word; Avalon would not let me do otherwise.

"If we meet with brigands," Thomas said as we left our camp, "I won't be of much help. It will be up to you. Stone them or something."

His wryness made me smile. "Don't worry. I will."

That day we topped the mountain pass. At the crown I managed to tug the black to a prancing halt, and Thomas pulled up the bay, and the two of us looked back into the misty distance behind us.

"I can't see the sea," I murmured. What I really meant was that I could not see Caer Ongwynn.

"It's still there," Thomas said.

Ahead of us, when we looked that way, lay the blue-veined plain I remembered from a long, boring ride in a canopied wagon when I was a child.

Odd. Scanning that waterscape, I could not find the castle I remembered. I could not see anything that looked like stonework or fortifications or even a village. Or a road. I could not trace where the path we were on might lead us. I saw no boats on the sky blue maze of streams. Except for a shadow in the distance like a green moon, a circle that might have been a mound or a ring of standing stones, I saw no sign that anyone mortal had ever ventured to Avalon.

"Downhill from here," Thomas said, then settled his feet deeper in the stirrups, swinging them forward to brace himself as we began the descent.

"I am not proud of the company you found me in," he said out of the blue. "That knight. I'm ashamed that you found me squiring for him."

"Why? Because he seized upon maidens?" I called over my shoulder to him, for the path was too narrow for us to ride abreast, and the black steed insisted on taking the lead. "Don't they all do that?"

"Not quite all. He had not done it before."

"Who was he? Sir Griffin?"

"No. I won't tell you his name. That way no one can surprise it out of you."

"I don't want to know it anyway," I grumbled, turning my attention to the path, now a ledge winding down the mountainside.

"Of course you don't," said Thomas placidly.

"I don't! I'm glad he's dead."

Silence while I thought how true that was. Killing the knight had taken less toll on me than healing Ongwynn had done. Murderous fury harrowed me less than love, it seemed.

This was not a comforting thing to think of myself.

Thomas said, "Anyway, I—when I entered his service, I didn't know. . . ."

I began to understand what he was trying to say. "Thomas, it's all right."

"No, it's not."

"Even True Thomas has to eat," I said. "Hush. Save your strength." I knew why he was talking about this now, and the knowledge chilled me: He thought he might not have another chance. He thought we might be riding to our doom.

He did not hush. "I had set myself a quest to find your mother," he said.

"And then you had to stop. It's all right."

"I did find out she was alive a few months ago."

I reined in the black and turned to look at Thomas, wondering why he had not told me this before. It should have been good news, but something in his voice told me otherwise. I nodded at him to go on.

"Redburke captured her first," he said, his voice and his

look as level as the plain below us. "She must have made her way back to Tintagel."

Probably trying to find Morgause and me. "And?"

"He used her hard, I hear."

At first I did not understand. I thought with a pang of Annie, of using her too hard, the sweat foaming on her flanks those first days of the journey. Then I caught the other meanings, and it was all the worse because I knew Redburke, his thick hairy neck and his turnip nose, and the idea, the image in my mind of his approaching my mother not as a queen but as a prisoner and a concubine—

I turned so that Thomas would not see my face and rode forward again. He said no more. He was waiting until I was ready to hear the rest of it.

"And then?" I asked presently.

"Penzance won her from Redburke, playing at dice—"

I clenched my teeth, and my legs must have clenched against the black charger also. He surged forward, almost pitching me off the mountainside.

"Morgan!"

"I'm all right."

"Stop that accursed horse."

I managed to wrestle the brute to a halt, turned to Thomas and said, "Just tell me where she is now."

"I don't know."

"Not at Penzance?"

"No. The story has it that he was sending her under guard to Caer Arienhrodd and she escaped somehow. The men-at-arms paid with their lives for losing her. Since then, nothing. She could be anywhere."

"Did she have food?"

"I don't know."

"A mount?"

"I don't know, Morgan. I'm sorry."

"Was this last winter?"

"Yes."

I nodded, nudged my horse with my heels and rode on in silence, thinking of Igraine the Beautiful alone and fleeing like a deer on the moor in the freezing storms that lashed up like a fist from the sea. My mother, facing mortal peril rather than facing one more day as a lord's—as a slave.

I said softly, "She might be dead."

We traveled late, under the light of a waning moon, for the tors dropped steeply and there was nowhere to stop until we had reached the foothills.

In the morning I awoke when the sunlight shone in my eyes, and I got up to see Thomas lying on the far side of a sheltering tree from me, still sleeping. I stood gazing at his face, fairer than that of any prince in any tale I had ever imagined, and I saw some color in his cheeks today, in his brow—

He stirred and gave a sigh almost like a moan, and I saw how his skin glistened with sweat. I stepped swiftly to him, crouched and laid my hand on his forehead.

Fever.

At my touch he opened his blue eyes and looked blankly up at me.

"Thomas, your arm, your shoulder," I said, "are they worse? Do they hurt?"

Looking too dazed to answer, he sat up, his face tightening—yes, he hurt. As gently as I could I slipped off his sling and removed his bandaging. The wounds had been healing well when last I had wrapped them, the morning we left our camp on the mountain—yesterday. It seemed long ago. Now Thomas's arm and shoulder were swollen and streaked with red.

"Contagion," I whispered, misery squeezing at my chest. Curses on me and everything about my harebrained journey. Annie dead, Thomas hurt, and now this. "Lie down, go back to sleep." I spun away and started rummaging in our baggage, my mind going like a squirrel, *flask of cold water, cloth of some sort, cold compresses, poultices—*

Thomas stood beside me. "Bind me up again and let's ride," he said.

"You can't ride!"

"Yes, I can."

"Thomas—"

"Just patch me together and put me on a horse! We can't stop now. We're almost there."

He could be very stubborn, my Thomas. So could I, but not this time, for the summons of Avalon sang to me like a harp string rooted in my heart, its pull stronger than ever. I could even sense the direction whence it came. It was as Thomas said, we were close. How he knew I cannot say. Thomas knew of many mysteries.

So we rode on, downhill and out of the forest and onto the plain, among a labyrinth of winding streams.

At the first stream I halted my horse and got down. Where the bank curved and a thick willow tree crouched over a deep pool, I knelt and soaked my shawl in the cold water. I pushed the cloth under the dark willow-shaded surface, and then, as I lifted it, dripping, I saw a face looking up at me.

A pale green face with hair that floated darker green, like waterweed. She looked at me with no expression, like an idiot, her mouth slack and lipless, her nose half eaten away by minnows. But she was not a corpse. Her pale, lashless eyes, one fishbelly white, one as brown as a tadpole, blinked and focused on me from under the water.

An odd calm came over me. I said, "Hello," stood up with my dripping shawl in my hands, and turned to Thomas—he sat on his horse in a near stupor; he had noticed none of this. I laid the sopping-wet shawl on his arm and shoulder, and with a corner of it I reached up to comfort his fevered face.

"I can do it myself," he mumbled, taking the wet cloth from me.

I, Lady Morgan, standing there in my sea green gown with my black charger's reins in hand—I confess I stuck out my tongue at him.

He smiled. "Let's ride."

The sun shone hot on the green plains of Avalon that day. A green-gold day, perhaps a trick of fate. The summons pulled me straight toward the green-moon place, the mound I had seen from the mountaintop, but the streams curved, curved, curved in the way, and the sun rays struck off their blue crescents like swords.

Within a few hours Thomas could no longer smile. He rode with his eyes half lidded against the glare and his own pain. I rode with mine wide open.

As we rode along one stream searching for a place to ford it, I saw what looked at first like a log of wood rise out of the water. It was the head of a black horse, its white-rimmed eyes watching me. Glinting eyes peered out of its flaring water-flooded nostrils as well. When my charger saw it, he shied so hard he almost threw me. I curbed him, and we rode on.

We rode through rocky shallows to cross. Nothing could harm us there, I thought. But when I glanced down, the water around the horses' hooves ran red, like blood.

There were the ordinary sights as well. Fish jumped, tall gray herons stood like druids in the shallows while in the deeper pools swans floated—

Wait. A white swan drifted as fair as the pearly moon, yet I stared, for on the surface of the water its reflection shimmered starry black.

I shivered with fear and wonder. But I said nothing to Thomas of anything I had seen, for nothing so far had offered to harm us, not the green woman who breathed water or the stream that ran red or any of it. Water, it all had to do with water, and I remembered a triad:

> *The gifts of the Mother are three:*
> *Fire that warms yet also burns,*
> *Tides that feed yet also drown,*
> *The flood that waters the Tree.*

When the sun stood overhead and beamed down most hotly, I called a halt. Thomas wanted to ride on. I took him by the waist and pulled him off the horse. He was so weak I could do that.

"Eat," I told him.

He could not. He lay flat on the ground under a willow tree

and did not move. I ate from the knight's provisions, cheese and siege bread, both as hard as Uther Pendragon's heart. I could not eat much. Worry for Thomas tightened my gut, and at the same time my hands trembled, my arms trembled, I quivered like a ringing bell pealing Avalon, Avalon, Avalon . . .

I thought of using the milpreve to cure Thomas, but I did not feel strong enough. This place of wild magic frightened me; what might happen if I succeeded only in hurting myself? Who would help Thomas and me then? Anyone? Or would some black horse spirit from out of watershadow pull us under and eat us?

Thomas was sleeping, or so I thought. I sat against the trunk of the willow, laid back my head, sighed and tried to close my eyes.

"Ride," Thomas said.

I helped him onto the bay, and we rode. We did not speak. Ahead of us I could see a great mound rising now, a green up-swelling like a woman's breast, like the breast of earth herself. The streams curved wider now, and deeper, and from one pool a slender white arm pierced the surface and stretched toward me, then sank with barely a ripple. I watched the water closing in from both sides, forming a sort of moat around the mound, leaving only a narrow approach. From the corner of my eye I watched Thomas, noting how his face paled, then flushed, then paled again, how he shivered with fever, how he fixed his eyes on his horse's ears and saw nothing else.

As the sun slipped toward the edge of the western sky I saw him falter, sway and grasp his horse's mane to keep from falling.

"Stop," I ordered.

He mumbled, ". . . almost there . . ."

It was no use trying to argue with him. I yanked the black charger in a circle to make it listen to me, urged it close alongside the bay, dropped the reins, put both arms around Thomas's waist and lifted him off the bay and onto my horse in front of me.

He struggled, of course, blast his stubborn pride. But he was too weak to struggle much. Within a moment he settled sideways between me and the pommel, laid his head on my shoulder and let go of consciousness and pain. I took the reins in one hand and let the steed set his own black-charger pace. The bay trailed along behind.

At sunset I rode into Avalon that way, on a black stallion with an empty mount trotting after me and Thomas unconscious in my arms.

11

IT WAS A CASTLE AFTER ALL. AND ALSO A LAKE. AND A great lofty mound. Avalon can be many places.

Here is how it was for me: I rode toward the mound with Thomas in my arms, and as the slanting rays of the setting sun touched the blunt stone at the apex of the mound and turned it golden, I felt a vibration like earth humming a primrose song and the mound bloomed open. The greensward parted like petals, lifted like leaves, and from within issued the warm light of many white candles in golden sconces, and I glimpsed the pillars and carved gilt groins of the great hall I remembered from years ago.

People, or perhaps I should say beings, moved about in the candlelight, but I saw only shimmers of them, for a man stepped forth to meet me. A tall, brown man, naked except for a deerskin. A man with a lined face and eyes like wells in forest shadow and the faerie sheen all over him. A man with the antlers of a stag growing out of his grizzled hair.

A fay.

That is to say, one who had been a god.

I halted the black charger, which for once seemed pleased to obey me; maybe the sight of the antlered god gave him pause the way it did me. From some long-ago triad in Ongwynn's tome of threes I remembered a name. "Cernunnos," I whispered.

> *Three there be who wear the horned crown:*
> *The moon white stag of the holy grove,*
> *The leaping hart of true love,*
> *And Cernunnos the antlered one.*

In the leaf brown depths of his eyes there showed a gleam when I said his name. "At your service, Lady Morgan." The shining tips of his antlers traced a hint of a bow.

I shook my head. Such a being could never be at my service. "Are you—was it you who summoned me here?" How otherwise did he know my name? But I remembered nothing of him in the dream, the sending.

"No. She's within." He walked forward to stand beside my steed and held up his arms to take my burden from me. His hands were all brown callus, I noted, grained like wood. On the third finger of his left hand he wore a ring that seemed made out of moonlight, and on the ring glimmered a blue stone. A milpreve.

I do not know why I trusted him, but I did. Utterly. Without question I lowered Thomas to Cernunnos, who cradled him in his arms like a baby.

By the time I slipped down off my steed, Thomas stood conscious and upright, gazing at me with dazed eyes, steadying himself with one hand on Cernunnos's shoulder. Healed. Or at least much better. But still weak and so bewildered that perhaps he did not realize what it was that he touched. Or what it was that had touched him.

"Thank you, Lord of the Beasts," I said to Cernunnos.

Again the shining tips of his antlers traced a hint of acknowledgment. "Who is this one?" Unspoken were the words: This is not one whom Avalon has summoned.

Thomas turned to look at Cernunnos, and his face went white. He tried to step back, but swayed as if he would fall. Cernunnos put out his harsh hand to support him.

Thomas moved his lips as if trying to speak, but he could not. I answered for him. "This is Thomas, to whom I owe my life. Will he—is he in peril here?"

"Perhaps. But peril comes from within the mortal heart. The pure of heart have nothing to fear."

"Then Thomas will be all right," I said.

I knew myself *not* to be pure of heart, not at all. I scorned my sister, I harbored secret thoughts of Thomas, and at heart I was no better than a seven-year-old jealous of baby Arthur, that same dragon of resentment still fiery in me. Too many times I had wished evil on others. The sheer power of my rage had killed a man. I was not a good person, I knew, so I felt more than a little fear as I walked into Avalon by myself.

I walked in between two pillars—the whole candlelit magnificence of that earth-dome castle stood open to the twilight summer air scented by water lilies. I stood hesitating and looking around—the many tables, the trays of sweetmeats and quail and marzipan, the candlelit throng were eerily as I remembered from that childhood day, years ago. But instead of king and lords and nobles and ladies, now I saw a laughing, feasting throng of—ladies? Goddesses? Women, at any rate, with not a man among them, women richly garbed and some gloriously ungarbed, old women and matrons and damsels and some maidens barely more than girls, queenly women and simple, pretty peasant women, some wearing the milpreve and some not, some with the sheen of faerie on them and some wearing a shadow I could not name and some as plain as Ongwynn. After three years with Morgause and Ongwynn and myself for company, I felt my heart lift and yearn at the sight of all those women so merry with nary a man to constrain them, so many that I could barely take them in with my eyes and mind.

None of them saw me or welcomed me, for I kept like a pisky to the shadows, shy. The primrose fay, I thought, was the one who had summoned me, so I scanned the hall for her—

I gasped.

At the circular table on the dais, straight-backed and staring down at her own white hands, alone within herself despite the maidens singing by her sides, sat a slim, regal woman with dark hair but a pale, pale face.

"Mother!" I cried.

My call echoed in Avalon's golden dome. I think every head except my mother's lifted or turned to look at me, but I did not care. Heeding no one's stares, I darted across the great hall to the table where my mother, Igraine the Beautiful, sat staring at her hands. I lifted my skirt and leaped like a boy onto the dais. I plunged to my knees by my mother's side.

Igraine the Beautiful—but the title was a mockery now. Every bone showed through her skin, lines harrowed her white face, streaks of gray sullied her long, limp hair, and her eyes stared as dull as a cow's.

"Mother," I appealed.

Her head turned slowly, as if fearing it might lose its balance on her narrow neck. She looked at me with vague surprise.

"Mother, it's me!"

"Morgause," she murmured.

"Morgan. It's Morgan, Mother."

She nodded as if it were all the same. "What are you doing here?" She leaned toward me, suddenly eager. "Did you bring Arthur with you?"

"No, I . . ."

"Oh." Plainly disappointed, she turned away.

"Mother." I scrambled to my feet, put my arms around her thin shoulders and embraced her and kissed her hollow cheek. But she seemed not to notice.

Someone touched my shoulder gently, so gently I hazily thought it was Thomas, even though Cernunnos had been showing him to a bath and a bowl of soup and a bedchamber the last I knew. But because I thought it was him, I turned without alarm.

It was she. The primrose fay with leaf-green eyes as deep as wells. Merry and sly and wise and sad.

I felt my knees weaken as if I should fall at her bare feet, but I did not. I only stood and stared.

"Come eat and bathe and rest, Morgan," she said.

I whispered, "My mother . . ."

The fay smiled, but there was more sadness than gaiety in

her smile. "Now you know why we summoned you," she said.

"Why me? Why not Morgause?" It was Morgause whom Mother seemed to want. Morgause more likely to be pure of heart.

The primrose fay's smile grew gay again, and mischievous. "You know why," she said.

I felt the milpreve stirring, warm with the heat of its own life, upon my chest.

"Thomas." I spoke softly, but when I caught sight of him, I broke into a run.

In an arbor by the water's edge, where the primrose fay had promised I would find him, he lay sleeping. Someone, Cernunnos probably, had seen to fresh clothing for him, and the arch of the arbor sheltered him, but he had no bedding. Perhaps he needed none, upon that soft green grassy bed. These fay folk seemed kind in their way. I had bathed, or rather I had been bathed most tenderly by the damsels of Avalon, my hair washed and scented and braided, and I had eaten, but I would not sleep until I had spoken with Thomas.

The dawn light gilded the grass on which he lay slumbering as deeply as if it were a bed of eiderdown. All was grass now; the mound of Avalon had closed behind me at the first touch of the morning sunlight.

"Thomas." I knelt beside him and touched his shoulder.

He opened his clear eyes. "Morgan?" He sat up at once, with no sign of pain, no sling or even bandaging any longer on his arm. "What's wrong?"

"Nothing. Everything. I don't know. Have you eaten?"

"Yes, of course." He paused, tilting his head as if listening to the echo of his own words, and smiled. "Yes, Cernunnos fed me well. Are they fattening me for slaughter?"

"I hope not." I sat down on the ground next to him. "That is what I want to tell you. Those knights who came here and—and were killed, or went mad . . ."

Tilting his head toward the mound, Thomas said, "Cernunnos has told me that no man is allowed within." He understood that much, then, that this was a place for women, ruled by women's magic, not like any other place anywhere that I knew of—but did he know what those doomed knights had done?

Or would he be safer not knowing?

Much more softly Thomas said, "Last night I saw the Morrigun crouching by the stream yonder." He looked a small way upwater of the arbor, where stones formed steps into a pool, where tiny ducks colored like jewels floated amid water lilies. In a tone oddly flat for him, Thomas said, "The Morrigun in her human form. She was washing the bodies of warriors who will die in battle."

I gawked at him.

"The water ran dark with blood," he added just as flatly.

I stammered, "Who—what did she look like?"

"She was just a hunched old woman keening like a ghost. But when she had finished she flew away in the form of a raven. I think it was a raven. Hard to tell for sure in the dark of the moon." He quirked his gentle smile at me. "Why are you surprised at anything that happens here, Morgan?"

135

I brought my faltering mouth under control, beginning to feel foolish that I had come running out to warn him. He knew more than I had thought. "Your arm—it's all healed?"

He nodded, raising it and smoothing the sleeve with his other hand as if to cherish it.

"Strong again?"

"Strong and not even scarred."

From the shade of the arbor I looked out upon sunshine and a plain like green velvet and our two horses, the scrawny bay and the sturdy black, grazing in the bend of a waterway. I blinked; in satin blue water the black horse cast a white reflection. In Avalon, I sensed, bright was dark and dark was bright. This was a place of warm light and cold shadow, peace and greatest peril. The black horse's white reflection glittered so much like a sword that I shut my eyes and shook my head.

"What?" Thomas asked.

"Nothing." I opened my eyes and did not look at the water again; I looked at Thomas. I swallowed, opened my mouth and made myself say, "You're strong enough to ride . . ." I ought to tell him to ride away to Caer Ongwynn, where it was safe.

"But I'm very weary. All I want is to rest."

I said nothing more. I could not. I did not want him to leave me.

"And you, Morgan?" He scanned my hair, my gown, with a shy wisp of a smile. "They welcomed you?"

I nodded, then blurted, "I—I suppose you're not in danger as long as you stay out here in the arbor. . . ."

He glanced behind him as if on guard, looking over his

shoulder at the mound of Avalon, breast of earth. He whispered, "Who are they who live there?"

"She," I said just as softly. "Women. Ladies. Fays. She, in many forms."

"Would you not speak in riddles?"

I gave up trying to explain and said plainly what I had come to tell him. "Those knights who died gave offense to her, sometimes only by a thought." And how was he to guard his thoughts even while he slept?

"Offense?"

I lowered my eyes.

He sat gazing not at the mound but at me, without speaking. He seemed to know that, as a maiden, I could say no more. "You're one of them," he said finally, "being woman."

"I—I'm not sure."

"It's because of the—the blue stone, then." He watched me steadily. "Or your changeling eyes. Something makes you one of them. That is why they summoned you here, is it not?"

"No." I shook my head too vehemently. "It's because my mother is here!"

Once again I failed to surprise him. He only nodded.

"You knew?"

"Cernunnos told me."

"Cernunnos this, Cernunnos that! Where is he? Inside? Why do they let him inside and not you?"

"Shhh!" Thomas stiffened and looked all around as if he feared Cernunnos might hear, although we could see for half a league in all directions: winding blue water, sunlight on the reeds, blackbirds whistling, golden fish, a white swan with a black reflection, the green mound with the standing stone on its apex, nothing more. Thomas told me softly, "You must not speak of him so freely."

"But he has been kind to you—"

"Morgan, there is danger everywhere. In Ongwynn. In you. Perhaps even in me. Certainly in Cernunnos."

"Would you not speak in riddles?"

Thomas smiled, sat with his back against a vine-wreathed pillar and told me what he knew of the Lord of the Beasts.

Cernunnos, the antlered consort of—the moon, the goddess, the dweller in Avalon. The one who was many, with many forms, many names. When the crescent moon lifted its two silver horns over Avalon, Cernunnos would go in to her. And under the full milky moon he would ride the nights on a white mare whose mane and tail trailed to the ground; sometimes he would ride as far as land's end. It was on such a night that he had found my mother crouching as wild and matted and louse-ridden as a starveling rabbit upon the moor, and it was he who had brought her to Avalon, where she was safe even from Penzance, even from Redburke. He had carried her there in his arms on a white horse.

But in the dark of the moon, Cernunnos rode a black steed with eyes that blazed like coals. On those nights he galloped with the fire-eyed pack, the hounds of the underworld, in their chase across the black sky as they chivvied the souls of the newly dead. Dwellers on the moors warned one another not to look up when they heard the yelping of hounds in the sky; those who witnessed that unearthly hunt ran mad.

As Thomas spoke of that uncanny ride, I shuddered and the day darkened in my sight. But then I blinked and looked around at bright sunshine, bright water, a white heron wading.

"Wasn't last night the dark of the moon?" I asked.

He nodded.

"I thought so. The Morrigun . . ."

"Yes." The Morrigun did her grisly washing in the dark of the moon. Thomas turned his eyes away from the mention of her name and said, "I'm weary, Morgan." He slipped sideward from the post against which he had set his back, and lay down in the grass again.

So was I, very weary, and too much in need of him to let myself know how much he was not saying. Within moments I fell asleep in the grass by his feet.

Only later, far too late, did I learn all that he had seen in that night of the dark of the moon. He had seen Cernunnos ride off upon the wild hunt, and he had not run mad, for Thomas was strong and pure of heart. If anything could drive him mad, it would have been this: Also that same night, he had seen the Morrigun washing a dead body he had recognized. It was his own.

12

"WHAT ARE YOU DOING?" I ASKED MY MOTHER, SITTING beside her in darkness lit only by a single candle.

She did not answer, only gazed upon the mirror—not the queenly silver mirror I remembered from when I was a child, but a smaller one, far plainer. It lay flat on the table before her, and the candle stood to one side, and Mother—had her back ever touched the back of any chair? Like a narrow pillar carved in the shape of a queen she sat, and it was as if she did not hear me at all. Why did I bother? Outside it was daylight. It had become hard for me to keep track when nights were bright and days dark and I wanted to sleep, but yes, it was day, and outside were Thomas and sunlight.

Yet I sat by my mother. "What are you doing, Mama?" I coaxed.

Perhaps it was because I called her Mama. I had never done so before. At first she kept silence as usual, but then she murmured, "Looking for Arthur."

I was woman enough now to sense how it might feel to have a child, a baby. For the first time I caught half a notion, not just a thought but a deeper knowledge, of what it might mean to be Queen Igraine, and pain squeezed my chest. "Oh," I breathed.

She whispered, "I want my son."

"Of course."

"They took him away."

"Yes."

"My son. My son. I must find him."

"But how . . . in the mirror?"

"Yes." She gave me a flickering glance. "Scrying. The fays taught me."

"They *did?*"

"Yes." She turned back to the shadowy mirror lying there like a silver pool, no, more like a well of water deep, deep, deep, only its surface glimmering in the candlegleam. "Arthur," she whispered.

"Do you see him?"

She shook her head just once, left to right and left again.

I asked, "Do you see anything?"

"Sometimes."

"What have you seen?"

She said nothing.

"Teach me to scry," I demanded.

She said nothing.

I moved my chair close to hers, so that I saw the mirror as she did, slantwise, with the candle out of my view. I sat as silent as she did, gazing.

Sleepy. I wished the mother-hunger in me would cease and

let me just go to sleep. My eyes blinked, but I willed them to stay open.

Teach me power.

This scrying, if it worked . . . What else might the fays teach Mother?

Or me?

Teach me power.

Maybe the reason I was here . . .

In the depths of the mirror, shadows swirled. I stared, without speaking, without moving, thinking hazily of the day I had dropped a dirty brown round thing in the washbasin and the dark covering had swirled and parted and I saw—not a blue stone this time, but a picture that seemed made of jewels and light. It was like seeing piskies, or so I would imagine seeing piskies, small yet oh so real. I saw Ongwynn standing at the hearth of Caer Ongwynn, and lovely Morgause sitting at the rude old table with a book in her hands, and on the table the chessboard, and sitting there—the other girl so much like Morgause, beautiful, yet so different, with a willful brow and the sheen of faery power all over her—and as I watched, Ongwynn spoke to the girls. I heard her as clearly as I had many times heard the piskies giggling. Ongwynn said, "I think both of you will need to live by your wits. Be secret and strong."

I gasped, and the vision shattered.

I babbled, "I saw—was that me? But that was months ago! Last winter!"

My mother did not move. "Arthur," she whispered, gazing at the shadowy mirror. "Show me Arthur. I want my son."

◆　◆　◆

"By what title may I call you, holy one?" I asked the primrose fay.

Splashing in a candlelit fountain that hadn't been there the day before, naked in the water with golden flowers and her own auburn hair floating around her, she smiled at me like a happy child. "You know my name, Morgan."

"But—"

"I daresay you know many of my names. Call me by any of them, Morgan, and I'll answer."

Sitting on the tourmaline stones at the fountain's edge, I knew I had to be careful. She was testing me. I had asked her name because I did not want to offend, but she had turned the question back on me.

And she was right to think that I knew her. I knew that she had been a goddess, or one face of the triple goddess; she was the maiden, the ever-crescent moon, the silver boat on a black sea, the springtime rose in bud.

I remembered the first triad Ongwynn had ever read to me. "Rhiannon," I said softly.

Her smile widened. "If I am Rhiannon, where is my silver bow?" Then she splashed water at me. "But you are right; that is one of me. What is it that you want of me, Morgan?"

I had not said that I wanted anything, but she knew.

I took a deep breath. "Teach me power," I whispered.

She laughed like the fountain chuckling, like silver bells ringing. "But power is everywhere, Morgan!" she cried, laughing, splashing. "You have only to learn!"

"But someone must teach me . . ."

"No one can teach you until you are ready."

"But I am ready!"

"Really?" She gave me her sweetest, most mischievous grin and tossed a golden blossom so that it hit me in the middle of my chest, leaving a wet spot on my silk-and-lace bodice. "Then why do you hide a pretty blue pebble under your gown?" She ducked beneath the surface of the water. For a moment her pearly nakedness shimmered in the fountain like dawn, and then she was gone. Where or how I did not know.

But why should anything surprise me in this place?

I sat where I was, staring at the water, not blinking, not really thinking, not even trying to scry—this was not a pool fit for scrying anyway, not smooth enough to show me reflections from afar, intimations of distant truths unseen. This was whispering water fluffed and ruffled by its own spray, scattering the light of many candles and the glint of many gilt pillars. Still, staring at that water, I caught a shadow somehow, an intimation of what I must do.

From under my gown I drew forth my milpreve dangling on its shabby cord. In the moon-silvered, candle-gilt, silken night of Avalon it shone like a steady blue star. No heat to it tonight, only an expectancy that was almost the same as happiness. It liked being out, finally, in the night air and the candlelight.

With the same cord I bound it to the third finger of my left hand, wearing it like a ring. Perhaps the fays would think me an upstart—or perhaps not. As soon as I had tied the stone in place on my finger, the ends of the old cord fell off, dropped into the fountain and swam away like eels.

The next dusk, when Avalon opened to the fragrance of water lilies, I left the candlelit hall and walked toward the arbor. Lying near the rushes that fringed the waterways, ducks tucked their heads beneath their jewel-colored wings to sleep. Rhiannon, or the presence I called Rhiannon, had given me a blue gown the colors of deep water in sunlight, a gown made of weightless gauze that floated and streamed and trailed in the soft grass around my bare feet the way my hair trailed around my bare shoulders. The druid stone on my finger lit my way in the twilight with a blue-gold glow.

I met Cernunnos walking toward me as he approached the mound, or hollow hill, or Caer Avalon, call it what you will. He walked tall, handsome, nearly naked, his gleaming antlers echoing the silver crescent in the sky. The consort, going in to his beloved.

The glow of his milpreve shifted as he lifted a hand to greet me. The starry points of his antlers sketched a bow. "Lady Morgan," he greeted me, glancing at the mystic stone displayed on my finger. "So you have decided? You will be a fay?"

I paused to look into his wise, not-quite-human eyes as I would not have dared a few days before, as I still might not have dared in daylight. "I must follow my fate," I said.

"But we all choose our fates, is it not so, Morgan?"

"I—I suppose so." It was a riddle worthy of the book of threes, but—yes, in a way I had chosen my fate the day I had healed Ongwynn.

"And choose, and choose, and choose again," Cernunnos said. "The time may come when you will choose to throw that away." He inclined his regal head toward my druid stone.

"No," I blurted, for I could not imagine throwing away my milpreve, the treasure that had come to me as a kind of recompense on the day my father had died, the talisman that had waited through millennia for me, Morgan. It was mine, mine alone, emblem and agent of my power to heal Ongwynn, my power to save Thomas—it was life to me. "No, I could never throw it away."

"Some have done so," Cernunnos said.

"But why?"

"Because, for a fay, there are ever harder choices," he said. "We all have shadows, is it not so? And we all must choose how to use our shadows."

I said slowly, "I do not understand."

"We all must choose whether to be content or unhappy. The ancient magic of the moon or the striving, aspiring way of sorcery."

I thought of merry Rhiannon with the druid stone banded on her hand, and of Merlin as I had seen him the night he took Arthur away, with just such a stone banded on his forehead above the black pits that were his eyes. I shuddered as Cernunnos saluted me once more and passed by. Surely I would never choose the way of sorcery.

With the grass soft under my bare feet and the springtime air soft on my bare shoulders and my magical gown soft around me, I walked on to the arbor. To Thomas. And my heart felt like water within me, for I knew that I loved him, and I knew that he must not love me. Not here, not in Avalon. In this holy dwelling of the moon mother, even a whisper of manhood might endanger him. So the fays had instructed me.

He sat at the entrance of the arbor watching twilight and candlelight play on the surface of the water. But when he saw me walking toward him with the milpreve glimmering blue on my finger, he rose to his feet, his face a white oval gazing at me, then knelt before me and bowed his head.

Who had shorn his hair? It was cut square in the shape of a helm, all the curl gone.

"Thomas," I whispered.

"Lady Morgan." He kept his eyes on the grass. He was wise, my Thomas, perhaps as wise as Cernunnos, with whom he had lately been conversing. Perhaps Cernunnos had instructed him as the women within Avalon had instructed me.

"Thomas, you must go from me," I said. Commanded, rather. And please, let him not raise his gaze to see how my heart was breaking, breaking, all made of salt tears like waves on the shore of Caer Ongwynn, so that in my weakness I might tempt him to his own doom. I told him, "You must leave Avalon. At once. Tonight."

He lifted pleading eyes, but looked down again quickly. "Lady Morgan," he requested, "if I must go—"

"You must." By Avalon's law, any man who desired a fay was desiring his way to death. This was a place of moon magic, a place of women's power, and all women know men live to take away such power. Love of a man weakens a woman, as Ongwynn had said.

I loved Thomas, and desire for him washed through me.

I told him, my voice not quite steady, "I am a deathly danger to you." I was Morgan le Fay, but I could not yet say what I might do, or might be unable to prevent. Morgan le Fay had been with me all my life, riding my chest, as near as my own heartbeat, yet she was a stranger to me.

"If I must go, Lady Morgan," Thomas said softly, "let me be your knight."

I stood not quite understanding.

Still kneeling, Thomas lifted his face to gaze up into mine.

And his face was lovely, so lovely, as pale and pure as the moon, and I thought I saw a single tear like a clear jewel below one shadowy eye. "Let me serve you as your champion, my lady," he requested. "Give me a worthy quest to sustain me while I am away from you."

I could not think. I could not imagine the future. I knew it might be years before I saw him again. If I ever saw him again.

Yet—could I not make it happen, that I would see him again?

Teach me power.

Power is everywhere, Morgan. Learn.

I was learning quickly. I nodded. I whispered, "Bring me your sword."

He fetched it from the arbor, and bowed again before me on bended knee. I laid the sword gently upon his shoulder. "Sir Thomas," I told him, my voice firmer now, "true knight of Avalon, arise."

He rose to his feet. For some reason I felt surprised that he stood taller than I.

"At your service, Lady Morgan," he murmured.

"You must go now."

"On what quest, my lady? To what purpose?"

To save his noble life? But I could not tell him that. I thought feverishly: purpose? Did his life have a purpose, or mine? For what purpose was I here? To become a fay? To save my mother?

"Seek my half brother who was taken away as a baby," I told him. "Seek Arthur."

He bowed. "I will be honored to do so."

"Thank you, Sir Thomas." My voice faltered. I turned away before he might see—

"Morgan," he said softly.

I stiffened. "Please go," I whispered, not daring to look at him.

"Take this to remember me by, Morgan, my heart. Please." He held out a small something toward me.

I took it blindly, then held it between both my hands, staring: It was a ring. A ring woven of his crisp black hair.

The night held its breath, waiting.

I slipped the ring on my finger. I breathed out.

"Farewell," Thomas said, very low, turning away.

"Wait." The word shot out of me, perilous. And still I could not look at him, for the tears I held back were more dangerous still. Quickly, he must be gone quickly. I stooped and plucked a violet from the grass, purple blossom and heart-shaped leaves and all. He had once said that my eyes were like violets at midnight, darkest green, darkest porphyry. I offered to him the little rag of a flower and whispered, "A knight needs a token." My voice trembled only a little.

Bless Thomas, he understood at once; he smiled. I will never forget that smile, brave and warm and innocent and— No. I must not see the rest. Must not see the yearning, the longing, the desire.

"Thank you, Lady Morgan," he said, taking the violet from me with a bow. "May all blessing abide with you while I— while I am away."

I nodded, no longer trusting my voice to tell him any of my whirling thoughts—go quickly, be safe, come back to me. I turned away from him and walked toward Caer Avalon, my head erect and my bare feet sure on the grass but my sight blurred by tears. I did not see him go.

149

13

AVALON OFFERED ME POWER AND PEACE. THE POWER I learned eagerly, but the peace I could not learn.

I could not even recognize it as the deep magic it was, peace everywhere in Avalon, in the glowing candlelight, the lilting voices, the calm dawns, the sunlit streams and calm pools. I could not see how peaceful were the streams that ran with blood from the Morrigun's washing, the pools from which green-faced women and black, horselike water devils peered. How these things swam in peace I did not understand.

Cernunnos tried to teach me such peace one day early in my stay at Avalon. That dawn I sat on the grassy bank of the pool near the arbor, weary yet not ready to sleep, missing Thomas, watching the swan float like a white feather-flower with its reflection mocking it, glossy black, on the winking water. What depths of mystery hid beneath that bright surface?

Staring bleary-eyed, I thought I saw an image of a towering

tree with white branches, living, moving—then I blinked and looked up. Cernunnos stood beside me.

"So, Morgan." He sat down on the bank with me, so tall that his antlers spread over my head. "What are you thinking?"

"This water frightens me," I said.

"She does? Ladywater? Why do you sit by her, then?"

I bristled, hearing a quirk of fun in his voice. "I am trying to understand!"

"Understand Ladywater? Impossible, Morgan. You can love her, and you can surrender to her as to fate, but you can never understand her."

I scowled, for I did not like his teasing tone or his words. "Surrender? What is Ladywater that she should have her way with me?"

He sobered. "Her way is the way of peace, Morgan. You are right to sit by her side. Hearken to her, and she will make you well and whole."

"I *am* whole!"

He neither smiled nor frowned. "Look at yourself in the pool."

Oh, for the love of mercy . . . but I did as he said, leaning forward to look down at my own reflection atop the winking water. I gasped. A plump middle-aged woman looked back at me, not just an image but a soul, as alive as I was, smiling at me with glinting serenity across a distance of time. I gawked at her. She seemed smug, like a kitchen cat, with bright predatory eyes, white-powdered cheeks, a rich rouged mouth. With a shock to my heart I recognized her, I knew her quite surely: myself. Morgan, in a few decades.

No. No, I did not want to be like that. I did not like her.

"Go away!" I exclaimed. Her smile widened, and the surface of the water rippled. She vanished from my sight. That was a long, long time ago. I remember looking at the black reflection of the white swan, then at Cernunnos, then at the water, which showed him truly, a harsh brown handsome man with the crown of a stag.

"Try again," Cernunnos told me.

"Try *what?*"

"To be whole, you must embrace her."

"But it's all a lie! I am not going to be like that!" I wanted to be loved, lovable.

"You must be all your selves before you can choose, Morgan."

I stared at him, feeling mulish and stupid. My look made him smile.

"You are woman," he said, not without reverence. "All the cycles, the phases of the moon are in you. Try again."

I sighed and looked again for my reflection on the water. And I did not find it. Instead, this time it was as if I looked up into sky instead of down into sunrise-lit water, and as if from far below I saw a great bird flying, a raptor the color of nightfall ashes with its head surrounded by a crown of azure light. I did not understand that blue halo, but I knew that dark, ominous bird.

"The Morrigun," I breathed.

Cernunnos said nothing.

"Me?" I looked to Cernunnos. "But how?"

"Fate?" He echoed my questioning tone.

"No. I'll not have it." I scowled. "Does this pool make such sport of everyone?"

"Everyone? Only a favored few come here, Morgan."

Then Thomas was numbered among a favored few. I demanded, "What would Thomas see in this pool?"

"Likely himself." But at the mention of Thomas, something eased and softened in Cernunnos, as if he felt the warmth of the rising sun.

"Himself, as in a mirror?"

"Look to your own wholeness, Morgan. You would like to help your mother, Lady Igraine, is it not so?"

I nodded. I wanted her to love me.

Cernunnos said, "But, Morgan, you can help no one until you are whole in yourself. Try again."

His tone made me want to shake him. I flared, "What about Merlin? The sorcerer, has he looked in this pool?"

Cernunnos stiffened. "Be careful, Morgan. Do not anger me."

The chill in his deep eyes made me flush and obey him at once, looking at the mirroring pool. And there, for a wonder, my own youthful reflection wavered on the surface. But then my face seemed to swim away like a trout, and I saw instead a Morgan blazing like fire, golden blue bright and breathing flame, a—a dragon? But I hated dragons, I hated the memory of Uther Pendragon's fiery dragon flag frightening me, a child, as he marched into Tintagel, driving my father's men prisoner before him. I blinked. The dragon eddied away, and there was—confound it, the powdered pussycat Morgan again, the pudgy middle-aged wench—

"Embrace her," Cernunnos urged, his harsh voice low and close to my ear.

Blast everything, I would show him. "Just so," I retorted, and I spread my arms and lunged. As I splashed headfirst into the pool, I thought I heard someone laughing, and I could have sworn it was she. The witch.

I encountered nothing weird or slimy underwater, blessed be. I kept my eyes shut tight, pinched my nose, kicked my feet against the bottom and shot back to the surface as quickly as I could.

Perhaps it was Cernunnos I had heard laughing. Certainly he was yelping with laughter as I rose from the pool streaming like a fountain.

"That was not what I meant," he gasped, laughing.

"Did I embrace her?" I challenged.

"I think you chased her away instead." As if my challenge were of no account, he offered me his hand to help me as I clambered out of the water. At his touch my clothes were dry again. "Very well, Morgan. I see you will learn wholeness in your own way, in your own time, if indeed you learn it at all."

He ambled away and left me, and I thought I had won. Not until eons later did I understand how much I had lost.

I sat by the pool again, gazed at the swan and dreamed of Thomas. Did he love me? Was I good enough?

I dreamed my way through that day and many to follow. Seasons passed like a dream in Avalon, like a whisper. The ducks would fly away, and sometimes there would be a lace-work of ice on the deep pools, gone before noon. Clouds like fish scales muted the sky and the sun set bloody, but Rhiannon still danced barefoot through longer nights until the ducks returned to nibble new grass so green it seemed to glow. Then everything would mellow for a timeless time, Cernunnos lazing in the arbor and Rhiannon bathing amid water lilies and my mother scrying by moonlight in the still pools and I tagging after all of them as pesky as a toddler, wanting to learn power like wanting to pull a buttercup out of the bud and make it bloom. Often the days and nights seemed very long to me, for I remained restless and uneasy within myself. Yet I lingered beside the waters of Avalon. And one morning the ducks would fly away again and the season turn, and another year was gone.

The ducks flew away three times. Three years gone by.

Eighteen years old now, I wore my milpreve on a band of orichalcum, the silvergold metal of the fays, magical metal I had melted and shaped with my mind. I knew the subtleties of scrying in metal or water; metal is like Redburke, remorseless and sometimes a trickster, whereas water is a kindly mother who sometimes wishes not to tell her children the whole harsh truth. I had neither surrendered to Ladywater nor embraced her, as Cernunnos had said I must, but it seemed not to matter. I knew how to heal all common ailments and how to bestow gifts and blessings and curses. I knew the languages of serpents and fishes and birds, although I spoke to them only haltingly. I had ridden on the milk white mare behind Cernunnos, and I had seen the mare take the human form of a goddess more lovely than Rhiannon, and I knew her name: Epona. I had played chess with that fearsome crone Menwy, and she had cackled like a heron when I was able to defeat her. I had seen the Morrigun at her washing, and I had seen the wild hunt that chivvies the souls of those who have died unforgiven. And I had lived. Slowly I had grown into a sense of what it meant to be Morgan le Fay.

Or so I thought.

And throughout that timeless time I had asked the mirror and the mirroring water for news of Thomas, much as my mother always and forever asked for news of Arthur. And I had sometimes seen a blond stripling whom I believed to be Arthur because the sight of him made my neck hairs bristle. But neither mirror nor moonlit pool had showed Thomas to me. I dreamed of him often, but the ways of dreaming are even trickier than the ways of scrying. I could tell little from my dreams except that Thomas was yet alive somewhere. I would have felt it in my dreams if he were dead.

Or the bronze mirror would have showed his death to me. That mirror had the soul of an earth demon, I think. Hateful. It showed me no lies, for it knew I had the power to blast it to bits, but it showed me much hurtful truth. Ongwynn growing old. Morgause growing lonely and bitter. Annie's death, again and again.

My father's death.

Even now, hundreds of years later, I can see it in my mind's eye as dagger-sharp as I saw it that day. In the candlelit bronze circle, shadows swirled and then there was my father riding, his visor raised so that I could see his face—how my heart sprang, leaping and trembling and floundering like a hart struck through by the hunter's arrow. I gasped for breath yet I could not turn away. I gazed unblinking at the image out of the past: my father, his gray eyes stern under his helm, his gloved hands strong on the charger's reins, his armor shining—and then he lowered his visor, and, thank mercy, I could not see his face as

156

he raised his sword, as—as he did battle. Even now that I have spread my fateful wings over many battles, I can hardly bear to think of that one, all darkness and moiling confusion and the screams of frightened men. I remember my father's shouts as they mobbed him and dragged him down from his steed. I remember his death scream.

And I saw what they did to him afterward.

I saw the battlefield, that dreadful garden of death, and my father's head on a stick like a scarecrow, and I remembered that other battlefield, and how I had cried on Thomas's shoulder, and how I had flung back my head and gazed into his grave, beautiful face and cried out my defiance of his fate.

From that day forth there began to grow in me a sense, a whisper, of what I, Morgan le Fay, meant to do.

But the conviction grew in me slowly, like a stream gathering its waters to become a river flowing. Slowly, for it would mean leaving Avalon.

If I had my way, fate be damned: Thomas would not die in battle. I would keep him safe with me always.

Before I could leave, however, I had to try to heal my mother.

I knew the task was likely to cost me dearly. Healing is a difficult, dangerous art with love at its heart. Because of the love, I had to be the one who tried; as a fay and as Igraine's daughter, I just might have the power to restore her. Perhaps not; hers was a stubborn malady. Cernunnos had tried to heal Igraine, and he had failed, although his power was great; I had seen it the day he had healed Thomas with a touch.

"Mother," I asked not quite idly, "do you remember what it means to be in love?"

She did not look at me or answer. In the three years I had attended her daily, nothing had changed: Igraine no longer beautiful, face like a skull, sat rigid, her scrawny back not touching the back of her chair. And she seemed not to know I was there. "Arthur," she murmured to the silver circle lying before her like a benighted pool.

"Mama." I used the word seldom, for it had a small power I wished not to wear away.

My mother glanced at me.

"Mama, what would it take to make you well?"

She shook her narrow head. "I am well," she whispered as if I had threatened her. She turned back to her scrying.

In the darkness under Avalon's dome I watched my mother, with a chill prickling my spine. What was it in Igraine that had defied the healing power of Cernunnos? And not only he. Many had tried, among them Menwy, Epona, Rhiannon—and if Rhiannon could not heal my mother, I knew I was an upstart and a fool even to think—

Now. This minute. I knew I had to attempt it at once, before my small courage left me entirely.

I stood, whispered a command to my milpreve—it blazed to life like a blue star—and I laid my hands one on each of my mother's rigid, brittle shoulders.

Had I known how much it would hurt, to no purpose, I might not have tried.

It was her pain that I encountered, such a knotted, stubborn, fearsome inward pain that I could not bear it, let alone budge it. Yet I experienced it through my hands clear to my heart, the power of that pain taking me over, when I would by far have preferred the fey power that had felled me when I had healed Ongwynn. The force of my mother's relentless suffering sent me staggering back, gasping and whimpering. Tears almost blinded me, but through the blur of misery I could see my mother sitting as before, staring at her mirror, as if she had not even felt my hands upon her.

I had managed not to scream, or not loudly, but somehow Rhiannon knew anyway and was there in an eyeblink, her arms around me. "Oh, Morgan," she whispered.

She smelled of waterflowers, as always. I laid my head on her half-naked shoulder and wept like a child, but within a moment the agony seeped out of me and my heartbreak turned to fury. As if I were still a six-year-old, that same old hateful fire dragon blazed hot, hot in my chest. I pulled away from Rhiannon and shouted through my tears, "She doesn't love me! She has never loved me!"

Rhiannon did not dispute it, but merely asked, "Do you love her?"

"Of course I do!" But I knew the moment I said it that it was not true enough, curses take it, and that was why I had failed. I did not love my mother as I loved Ongwynn. It would have been more true that I wanted Mother to love me, to think of me, to ask for me and not always and forever that hateful Arthur, Arthur, Arthur.

"Arthur," my mother murmured yet again to the shadowy mirror. "Show me Arthur."

"Maybe it's not so simple," I told Rhiannon wearily.

"Is love a simple thing?"

I shook my head. "It's no use for me to try again."

"Perhaps in another season or two? You are still very young."

I lifted my eyes to hers, feeling spent enough to tell her plainly, "I must leave soon."

"Morgan! But why?"

Love, murmured the shadowy river of self gathering within me, growing, starting to sing. *Love always and forever, never to be lost.*

To Rhiannon I answered only, "I have plans."

Still, I might have lingered a while longer, for time meant little in Avalon, and a morning beside those shadowshining waters passed like a moment—but the very next day, Ladywater herself set spurs of fear to me and rushed me on my way.

I remember as if it were yesterday: I walked barefoot through rank new grass, wild with buttercups and bluestars, to the swan pool. I sat on the grassy bank in the sunshine, thinking of nothing but Avalon's beauty; how could I leave this place of wonders? But then in the mirroring water I saw an image of Ongwynn lying white-shrouded amid wreaths of columbine.

Dead.

My heart went numb. I sat without moving or speaking as the image rippled away and the white swan drifted past, its black reflection turning its graceful head to look at me.

The message was kindly meant, I knew. This was Ladywater, the very tears of the great mother. She would not show me anything to hurt me unless she had a reason.

Columbine. Ongwynn was fated to die in the early summer. I had time.

Motherwater had showed me to give me time.

It was time to leave Avalon. Time to go home.

"Mother," I told Igraine, "I don't know whether I will ever see you again."

She did not look at me. "Arthur," she murmured to the mirror.

I hugged her around her narrow shoulders, kissed her cheek—cool and withered, like shirred silk—and turned away.

I had already said good-bye to the others: Rhiannon, Epona, Menwy, and many whom I have not named. I did not turn back now, could not turn back. I raised my head and stiffened my spine.

The petal-portals of Avalon were just closing as I strode outside, where in the dawn light Cernunnos awaited me beside a caparisoned steed pulling at its reins.

I did not ask him where he had procured that grand horse for me. I knew that sometimes false-hearted knights were still foolish enough to venture to Avalon.

"Thank you, my lord." I bowed my head to him and sketched a curtsy of sorts—I wore the clothing of a lady again, or approximately so, with a mantle around my shoulders and a heavy skirt flowing to my feet, and I gave him the courtesy of a lady. But he surprised me. He hugged me, and my heart swelled when I felt the warmth of his embrace; I returned it, laying the side of my head for a moment on his brown-furred shoulder.

"You know you are not yet whole," he said. "You have not embraced your shadow."

I pulled away from him, harrowed by the memory of shadows in the mirroring pool: the matron and the crone. Age and death. A sorceress and the Morrigun. I flared, "I will never embrace."

"Do not say that! You do not yet know; you are a young moon just rising. Do not yet set yourself to battling the tides."

Nonsense, I thought. I felt that I was ready and equal to all that I planned to undertake. But I said nothing, only looked into his face.

Under his crown of antlers his deep brown eyes, shadowed like forest pools, gazed back at me. "You have not yet come to the choice," he told me.

The choice of which he had spoken that first day, between the peaceful ways of fays and the shadowed ways of sorcery.

"How can you say to embrace, then say to choose?"

"You must *be* to choose who you will be."

"But have I not chosen to be a fay?" I argued. "Why would I choose an evil path?"

"Not so much evil as . . . restless, discontent, out of tune with the cycles. Estranged from the mothers." As he spoke, his eyes blazed golden, so hot I stepped back. "Trying to be a lord over the earth. Apart."

I understood much that he was not saying, would never say: that he had been a god, like the others, whereas a sorcerer like Merlin only aspired to be a god. Estranged from the ancient power of earth, Cernunnos had said. It was in the cycles of earth and moon that Cernunnos and the fays found life and strength. I asked, "From what do sorcerers draw their power, then?"

Cernunnos gave me a long look, the golden fire in his eyes dimming to a gentle glimmer. He answered quietly, "From self-will such as yours, Morgan."

My heart burned dragonish with vexation. I wanted to breathe fire at him, and I could have done it, but I stamped my foot instead. "You think I will be that sorceress I have seen in the pool? Never! I hate her!"

Cernunnos only sighed, then smiled upon me, wistful and wry and not quite human. Without another word about wholeness or choice or fate, he helped me onto the charger and handed me the reins. "May the Lady give you a safe journey, Morgan," he blessed me. "Farewell."

I hated him. I adored him. My feelings battled within me so fiercely that I could not speak, but I lifted my hand to answer his blessing and bid him good-bye. Then I turned the steed toward the mountains and let it carry me away as fast as it liked. And so I departed from Avalon.

I stopped only to sleep or wash my face and once to lay blue windflowers on Annie's cairn. That foul knight's armor still lay over her where I had piled it, and his whitening bones lay amid rotting woolens nearby. Odd that nothing had been disturbed.

I knelt there a moment by Annie—what was left of Annie—then rode on.

Three times by then I had met with knights errant, but I had not troubled myself to hide from them; I had stared them down. It was not the usual thing for a girl of eighteen to ride alone, on a war horse, wild-haired and astride, with a split velvet skirt flowing down over spurred boots and a blue stone flaring with its own fey light on one finger—not usual at all. Perhaps it was my defiant strangeness that gave them pause. Or perhaps it was the way I could control the charger with a touch or a thought, with no need of bit or reins. And no need of a pack horse, for fays have ways of procuring what they require. Perhaps those knights whispered to themselves, "Fay." Perhaps they saw my uncanny eyes, or—of course there was the shimmer of faery power all over me; I am always forgetting that. No wonder they growled in their beards and let me alone.

And likely they spoke of me to those whom they met: Did you see her? Who was she? Where did she come from? Where is she going?

None of this frightened me, although it should have.

And so kicking up rumor like dust wherever I passed, I scaled the tors and cantered curveting through the villages and let my courser gallop across the moors and journeyed swiftly to Caer Ongwynn.

BOOK FOUR

Caer Morgana

14

I CLATTERED IN JUST AT SUNSET, AMID PEACH-AND-purple light glancing off the billows of the sea, and my noise brought Morgause out of the portal. She wore one of the gowns I had left, in ruins now, and her hair hung in a long frazzle, echoing—lines on her face? But she was only nineteen, a year older than I. How could she be so worn?

At first she gawked at me—I think in the sharp-edged light slanting off the sea she could not at once tell who I was. Then her taut face twisted, and she shouted, "High time you came home!" as she burst into a spate of tears. As I jumped down from the charger, she strode over and hugged me hard, then pulled back as if she wanted to slap me. "Morgan, you are so beautiful. Do you have a sweetheart? I hate you. Where is Annie?"

"Dead," I said as gently as I could, and still my voice came out with an edge. "My fault. Ongwynn?"

Morgause went very still, her wet, weary face trying to spare me.

Columbine; Ladywater had shown me Ongwynn's body draped with columbine. And columbine would not be in bloom for a month yet. Ongwynn could not yet be dead. Must not be dead. I asked, "She has taken to her bed, is that it?"

My sister nodded.

I reached up and touched the horse in the middle of its forehead to tell it not to wander, left it standing in its gear and strode into Caer Ongwynn.

It was dim and smoky in there, with the chill salty air seething in the ivy-mantled wind holes just the way I remembered. Peat piled by the hearth, onions hanging in bunches, chickens scratching at the dirt floor—nothing had changed at all. Yet all seemed petty, rude and strange to me, perhaps because I was a fay now and accustomed to the grandeur of Avalon—or perhaps because one thing was greatly wrong. Ongwynn's bed stood before the hearth, and she lay in it, and the very stones of Caer Ongwynn mutely wept.

Ongwynn. I stood for a moment by her bedside gazing down at her face—lidded eyes, silent mouth, a face as simple and stolid as a water-sculpted stone. "Nurse?" I whispered.

From behind me Morgause said, "She can't hear you anymore."

I sat down on the edge of the bed, put my mouth to my hand and thought a wish to my milpreve and kissed it, then laid that hand to the side of Ongwynn's still face. "Come, weary one, wake up for a moment," I murmured.

Ongwynn's eyelids fluttered. She opened her eyes and gave me a placid tan look. Her mouth stirred; she smiled at me. "Morgan," she murmured, "you're back. Good."

From behind me Morgause gasped. "Can you—Morgan, can you heal her?"

"No." Ongwynn spoke before I could, her voice like a whisper through dried grass. "It's my time."

Without turning—for I wanted to look only at Ongwynn—I said to Morgause, "Cernunnos has spoken for her. And somewhere a baby girl has been born who will be the next Ongwynn."

"And you, little Morgan?" Ongwynn spoke like a breath of west wind. "Who will you be?"

I knew who I *was*—Morgan le Fay. But somehow that was not the answer to Ongwynn's question. I did not answer. I turned to give my sister a look over my shoulder and said, "It is you whom I can heal." This I knew was true, for I loved her in my way.

But once again that tearful anger spatted out of her. "I don't want your pity! And I don't want to stay here with you. While you have been traipsing about dressed in grand clothes, I've been rotting here—"

"Shhh!" I darted a look at Ongwynn to see how she was taking this. But she had closed her eyes again. Perhaps she did not hear. I hoped not.

Morgause ranted on. "—an old maid rotting away, year after year, for I've lost count how many years—"

"Hush." What she was thinking, saying, did not trouble me; like her, I had mostly forgotten why we had fled to Caer Ongwynn in the first place: to hide from Redburke. But surely he had forgotten all about us by now. Morgause could go away if she wanted; fair was fair, and also in accord with my plans—

except that I did not want Ongwynn to hear her and be troubled. I stood and laid my hand to the side of my sister's face. Her eyes opened wide, and her lips softly parted. She hushed.

An old maid at the age of nineteen? The world might think so, but we of Avalon thought differently.

"Ongwynn is ready to let go," I told Morgause softly. "It will not be long now. You will want to stay just a little while longer, won't you?"

She nodded.

"And then you may venture forth to find—to find your heart's desire." As I spoke I stroked her face, soothing away the lines; in a moment they vanished as if they had never been. I caressed her hair, and the tangles fell away so that her tresses hung smooth and lustrous once more. I smoothed the worry out of her forehead, coaxed color back to her skin. I smiled, and saw an answering smile put the light back in her eyes.

"You are very beautiful," I told her, for it was now true; she was my all-too-lovely sister Morgause again. "Go and rest, think about nothing. Sleep. I will keep watch."

And so I did, after I had seen to my horse; I kept watch over Ongwynn throughout the night, for my years at Avalon had accustomed me to going without sleep.

And during that night, as Morgause slept and Ongwynn lay silent without even snoring, as darkness lay silent and even the piskies tiptoed about their business without chuckling or rustling, during that night of the swelling moon, the plan within me grew to fullness like Epona's belly and spilled out of my heart into my mind and my hands. And the druid stone yearned Indy blue on my left hand, and the ring Thomas had given me, the ring made of his curling black hair, shone like midnight on my right hand, and my heart yearned, and my mind knew what to do. I got up, took off the ring made of my mother's hair and placed it on the mantel over the fireplace, for it had grown frail, and I would wear it no more; I would put it in a chest for safekeeping. Then I stood in the middle of the room under the stone dome, and slowly turned so that I faced the North Star, then the sunrise, then the Archer, then the sunset and the North Star again. And as I turned the full circle of the world, I closed my eyes, laced my fingers together over my heart, and with one fingertip I stroked the milpreve and with another fingertip I stroked the shining sleek hair that had come from Thomas's head. And as I touched the rings I gathered all the power that was in me and gave it forth in a sending.

For I am Morgan le Fay, and it was in my power to summon him to me.

I gave forth a sending for Thomas.

Dying has its own rhythm and its own sweet time, just as living does. During those days and nights of the waxing moon I sat by Ongwynn's bedside and burned windwort to ease her breathing and rubbed her cold hands and sometimes read to her from the book of threes:

> *In the knot of fate there be three strands:*
> *One of a blackwing weaving made,*
> *One of the blackthorn heart of a maid,*
> *One not to be found in the Morrigun's hand.*

"What does that mean?" Morgause whispered, kneading bread at the table nearby.

"Nothing I can say." The triads meant anything only slant-wise, like scrying—and the thought made me put the book aside and pull from my pocket a circle of silver, a mirror. I laid it on the table at arm's length from Morgause, so that the hearth fire lit it darkly, and I asked her, "What do you see?"

"Oh!" She gasped with delight and reached for the mirror with her dainty white-floured hand, but I stopped her.

"You'll get to admire your lovely face soon enough," I chided. "What do you see—"

But there was no need to say more. Her eyes widened, and following the direction of her gaze, I saw the shadows swirl and part, and then I saw a knight riding—no, a king, for above his bearded, dark face glinted a heavy crown. "He," Morgause breathed. "Riding out of the north." And indeed the North Star glinted over his shoulder.

"You have seen him before?"

"In my—dreams . . ." My sister's voice faltered. Then she blurted, "Is he real, Morgan?"

"Oh, yes." The silver mirror showed nothing that was not real—although it might show something long past, or yet to come. I whispered a small spell to keep the vision in place in the mirror, then turned to the hearth fire and picked up an ember in my hand.

"Morgan!" Morgause cried, grabbing at me to stop me.

"It's all right. It does not hurt me." I placed the glowing coal on the mirror, squarely upon the vision's kingly face. The ember flared into flame, then flickered out and fell to ash. Under the ashes the king rode on. "Blow upon the ashes," I told Morgause.

"What? Why?"

"Just do it. Try to blow them off the mirror."

She leaned over the mirror and puffed. The ashes stirred, but only to form letters, a name: LOTHE.

"King Lothe of Lothian," I murmured, for I had heard the name. Far to the north his kingdom lay, and like many other petty kings he warred for the throne Uther Pendragon had left empty.

He rode into the distance, a tiny, manly figure amid soot and shadow, as Morgause gazed upon him. Then the mirror darkened and he disappeared. From somewhere far up in the chimney stones a pisky chuckled, and the ashes swirled and flew in my face, making me cough.

"Stop that," I grumbled.

Morgause picked up the mirror and held it between her two faltering hands as if she feared she might drop it.

"Yours," I told her. "Use it in good health."

I could tell by her wide, dreaming eyes that she could barely speak. She nodded and clasped the mirror to her bosom as if it were a lover.

"You'll be needing some comely gowns," I teased her. "You can take mine. Or perhaps the piskies—"

On her warm bed by the hearth, Ongwynn stirred and murmured. I stooped over her and touched her forehead—cool to my touch, like summer stone nestled amid moss and fern.

"Morgan," she breathed without opening her eyes.

She wished to speak. I sat on the edge of the bed, whispered to my milpreve and laid my hand against Ongwynn's temple to give her strength. Her pebble brown eyes opened and fixed on me.

"Morgan," she murmured, "Morgan spreading your wings, beware."

Something in the quality of her gaze turned me to a child again. My hand clutched at my chest. "Beware—beware what, Nurse?"

"Heart of a maid," Ongwynn whispered.

"Oh." Black wings, blackthorn heart of a maid. I breathed out. "The triad I was reading, that's all." But at my back I felt Morgause's utter silence.

"Playing," Ongwynn mumbled. "Little Morgan playing with the missing strand, playing with fire. Careful, child. Careful." Her eyes closed again and she lapsed into stupor.

"The sheen's all over you," Morgause whispered, "and great shadows rising from your shoulder blades."

I stood up and shook myself. "Bah." I strode outside, breathing deeply of the night air. By the spring pool, place of peace, a fallow doe and her two fawns gazed at me with wide shadowshining eyes, then drank on. I sighed and looked up at the nearly full moon and thought of Thomas. When would he come to me?

Columbine bloomed first. I had said to Morgause nothing of my vision for Ongwynn, but on her own Morgause went forth to the rocky moorlands where columbine grew, then came into the hearth room with her arms full of vines in sweet-scented, soft-purple bloom. Sitting at Ongwynn's bedside, she looped the columbine into wreaths.

"Ongwynn, can you smell it?" she whispered, hanging swags of columbine on the bed, the hearth, the chimney.

"Can you see it? Isn't it pretty? Morgan, look! See, she smiled!"

I nodded. "She knows," I managed to say past the lump in my throat.

The columbine blossoms wilted during the day and closed at dark, but their scent lingered. And in that fragrant moonlit night, Cernunnos came for Ongwynn.

He did not enter. Rather, one moment Morgause and I sat in a hollow hill, the domed stone room empty except for Ongwynn's labored breathing, and the next moment—immense, his presence filled Caer Ongwynn, the great tree of his antlers spreading to the walls and ceiling, the white tines scraping the stone. Morgause gasped and whimpered; I grasped her hand to still her. His naked shoulders furred like a stag's, Cernunnos looked down upon me without apparent recognition.

"We are honored, Lord of the Beasts," I said softly, for folk died commonly but few went with Cernunnos. Most were chivvied by his hounds.

He gave a curt nod, reached for Ongwynn, gathered her up, blankets and all, as easily as if she were a swaddled baby, and cradled her to his great chest. In that moment the sound of her breathing ceased. In the next moment he faded like fog and disappeared.

Hauling Morgause by the hand, I darted outside. The moon floated like a water lily in the dark sparkle of starlit sky, and across that great blossom of moon rode Cernunnos upon the milk white mare, his antlers shining, Ongwynn cradled to his chest, his black hounds pacing quietly at his mount's heels.

"Ongwynn is indeed greatly honored," I said. No wild hunt

for her, no bared fangs, no snarling beasts pursuing her soul, no pleading and terror. Hers would be an afterlife of peace and rest.

Cernunnos turned his antlered head slightly, perhaps looking back at us. By my side, Morgause gave a choked sound and fell down in a faint on the ground.

15

A WISP OF DECRESCENT MOON HUNG IN THE DAWN SKY.
"Like a curl of Ongwynn's hair," Morgause said, fastening the packs behind her saddle.

"Yes," I murmured, crouching by the spring pool to fill Morgause's flask for her. Indeed, Ongwynn's hair had grown wispy fine and moon white those last days, and now everything reminded me of her, the placid face of the pool, the dawn sky translucent and veined with smoky blue like the thin pulse at her temples—

"Is she really dead?" Morgause asked. "It is hard to believe she is dead."

I studied the white sickle floating like a swan's pinfeather on the dawn-lit surface of the pool, then dipped the flask, scattering the illusion. Even though the day would be fine and hot with a blue June sky, I shivered in the dawn damp and the breeze blowing chill off the sea, as always. "She is gone," I said. "It is hard on us. But she knows no hardship now."

"I should have snipped a lock of her hair," Morgause said. "Something to remember her by."

I remembered how long it had taken me to feel in my heart that my father was dead. No grave, no body to wash, nowhere to lay flowers. That was what it had been like for Morgause the past week or more gone by. There had been Ongwynn's bed to put away, her few woolen robes to wash and fold and lay in chests, wreaths of withered columbine to be pulled down and burned at the hearth. Then, nothing. Some weeping, some talk, but nowhere to place Ongwynn's passing and lay it to rest.

I rose and gave Morgause the flask. "Remember her when you look at the moon," I said. "Are you ready?"

Without answering, Morgause turned to scan everything around her: dawn, sea, shore and moor, spring pool and garden and lambs and hens and the ivy-draped dome of Caer Ongwynn. Her horse, the sturdy charger I had ridden here, pawed at the turf, eager to be gone. I had taught her a few clumsy charms to protect herself from knights errant, brigands, anyone who might wish to harm her on her way, simple magics such as even a mouse like Morgause could learn. And the piskies had gifted her generously with provisions, a purse of gold, gowns worthy of a queen; her lovely face looked back at me from under a headdress of velvet and gold and white linen.

"What is going to happen, Morgan?" she whispered. "What will become of us?"

I felt myself smiling. A year my elder, Morgause still looked to me for her answers. "I am a fay," I chided, "not a seeress."

"But—but you know so much. Shadows always moving in those star-crossed eyes of yours."

"I am not cross-eyed!"

"You know what I mean."

I rolled my insulted eyes and shook my head. I did not like to say anything, for Morgause took my every word as a promise, but to humor her, I said, "I imagine you will find your precious King Lothe. I hope you will like him, especially if he wants to wed you. Or would you rather stay here?"

"You know I can't."

I knew she would not want to. Nor did I wish it.

Morgause sighed, smiled, gave me a long embrace and kissed me, then turned to her steed. With my hands I made a step for her to mount by. Then I stood back. "Do you have the ring Mother gave you?"

"Yes. Next to my heart." Morgause lifted the reins, arranging them in her kid-gloved hands. The steed danced in place, but still she did not let it canter away.

"Morgan," she appealed to me, "are you sure?"

"Sure of *what?*"

"What—whatever mischief is in your eyes! Whatever you're going to do, what Ongwynn tried to warn you against—"

I had spoken to her nothing of my plan, and certainly I had not thought she could see it in my eyes. "Just go," I ordered her. "If King Lothe comes here before you find him, I will marry him!"

"You'd better not!"

"Then you'd better get going, hadn't you?"

"Contrary wench. I hope you grow a wart right on the tip of your ugly nose."

"It is not ugly!"

"Is so! My sister the witch!" Smiling at last, Morgause loosened her reins. The steed sprang away.

"Milkmouth!" I yelled after her. "Dairymaid!"

She waved, then cantered over the hilltop and disappeared. Even though I could not see her, I stood looking after her for a long time.

Then I wandered down toward the sea, whirled to spread my skirts around me and sat cross-legged in the coarse grass at the edge of the gravel beach. Most of the day I sat there listening to nothing but the echoes of my own emptiness. At first I drew circles with my fingertip in the gravel and sand. Later I pulled from my head three strands of my long, sable brown hair, each strand so long that by plaiting and weaving just the three of them together I made another circle as slender and shining as a wedding band: a ring for Thomas.

That evening I sat alone by the hearth and said to the emptiness that was Caer Ongwynn, "Come out, you."

I heard a startled squeak, then a chorus of giggling. I did not smile.

"Come out," I repeated levelly. "I wish you no harm; I know how long and well you have befriended me. Come out."

Now there was silence deeper than the sea.

I said, "I wish to see you and speak to you. All of you. Come here before me."

Silence deeper than sky.

I fingered my druid stone ring and tendered it just a silky stroke or two, like touching a newborn. I told the denizens, "I have no wish to distress you or hurt you. Come out, now. Take your time." I continued to give the milpreve a slow, soft stroke, then a moment's pause, then another stroke.

Shrill voices chittered, clamoring like mice, and in the corners shadows darted and milled. Little by little, gently, with just the power of one careful fingertip, I gathered them toward me. Dragging their bare brown feet they came, some falling to their bony knees and bracing their knobby fingers against the stone, some squealing like hedgehogs, so that my heart misgave me. But it had to be done if I was to be mistress of Caer Morgana.

At last they all stood before me plain to see in the light of the hearth fire, just a rabble of tiny skinny brown folk, naked, of course—just as a pedlar cannot heal herself, brownies and piskies and the like clothe their betters, not themselves. Naked, dirt-colored, homely if not downright ugly, they pouted at me like bony babies, some of them glowering, some weeping. "Shhh," I coaxed. "It will not be so very different than before. Tell me your names."

"No!" cried one who looked like a big-eared lad with a scraggle of brown beard starting on his pointed chin. "No, we canna! You'll make us all your slaves."

"You'll be my servants," I agreed, "but cherished, not enslaved. You can tell me your names, or I can give you names. You'd rather be called by your own names, wouldn't you?"

Some, mostly female and less defiant, named themselves to me: Willow, Heartsease, Crimson, Root, Gilly. Others I named: Puck, Wisp, Mandrake, Winkle. As they named themselves or as I named them, I took them one by one in my hands. At my first touch each of them shivered like a baby hare lifted from the nest, but then grew very still, hearkening to my hands as I stroked their small bodies taller to about half human size, stroked their hands and feet and features finer and less brown, more the color of a fallow fawn, then stroked fine blossom-colored clothing onto them. They liked it, I think. "Willow, what color shoes do you want?" I would ask. "Red? Yellow? A green cap? White owl's feather?" And sometimes one of them would murmur a reply. I gave flaxen hair to one. Hazel eyes to another.

When I had finished, they surrounded me to the reaches of the hall, a crowd of servants waiting to do my bidding.

I told them, "True Thomas is coming."

They faced me soberly, their great brown eyes intent on my face.

"I have summoned him," I went on. "I feel him approaching." In my dreams and sometimes in daylight, in a flash of vision, a glimmer in the surface of the pool, an intimation glimpsed in the shadow of a cloud—in many ways I felt him riding nearer. And I felt the hardship of his journey—hunger, nights of cold and rain, sometimes robbers or worse foes to fight. "He is not too far from here even now, even as I speak. But he is very weary."

They chirruped and murmured sympathy for True Thomas. Of course they knew him. They knew True Thomas perhaps better than I did.

"He has almost lost heart," I told them. "I want for him only rest and peace and happiness when he comes here. I want to make Caer Morgana into a paradise for him."

Now they chittered and rustled among themselves, their whispers rising to a clamor of excitement. I smiled. It was as I had thought; what they might do only grudgingly for me they were more than willing to do for him.

"A paradise," I said. "And a place of safety." This was the most important part. "It is for this that I have taken you into my hands: I shall make Caer Morgana into a stronghold that cannot be breached. No sword must ever slash Thomas, no pike run him through; True Thomas must never die in some lord's petty war. Never. He must live to be old, older than Ongwynn. I love him." I was not afraid to say this out loud, although I should have been, I should have known how dark wings flew silently overhead in the night. "I love him truly; I have loved him since I was a child. And this one love of my life I will keep forever safe from harm."

A chorus of squeaks and squealings rose. Bless the little ones, they were cheering.

Within a few days Caer Morgana rose from what had been Caer Ongwynn. Where there had been a hilltop now there stood a domed palace magicked out of honeysuckle and sea foam, sunset gold and my memories of Ongwynn's smile. Witchcraft, thought the shepherd lad who first saw it and ran to tell the distant crofters. Witchcraft, magic, illusion, thought the few hardy villagers who came to gawk—but magic is neither witchcraft nor illusion. True magic is made of love, not witchery, and it is more real than real, more solid than stone, for only a greater magic can breach it. This I had learned during my seasons at Avalon. The onlookers were kept back by walls they could not even see, invisible battlements as stubborn as stone, made of my own willful love, manned by sentries who never slept—black-feathered soldiers all named Rook. And a river flowed down now, my life my love my heart's blood, deep and impetuous it streamed down and embraced Caer Morgana with its protection then plunged into mother sea. Within the encircling walls and white water, the wellspring sparkled brighter every day, the still pool spread wider, the bittern stood motionless and wide-eyed in the rushes by the verge, and the rushes gave forth lavender-and-white blossoms with the sweetest fragrance I have ever known. In the mirroring silver water, the blossoms nodded velvet purple, and where ivy wreathed the dome, in the pool I saw golden filigree.

Ladywater. The very tears of the mother of us all.

Throughout the days of these transformations I sat by the pool, my skirts a circle around me, my fingers stroking the circles of my rings, my thoughts and dreams circling out farther to encompass river and walls and domed keep, and what I dreamed into being, my servants tended and cherished. Only the pool itself I could not and did not change and make my own, for Ladywater flows by the hidden ways from Avalon.

I would not have put a border of amaranth and moonstone around the springwater pool anyway. I loved it as it was.

On the day all seemed completed, I sat by the pool and gazed at the shadowshining water and let my musings make sure that all was ready, my fingers idly fondling the ring made of Thomas's hair, my thoughts eddying like white water, my dreams circling out, out, reaching—

Shadows swirled just beneath the mirroring surface of the pool, and for a moment I stopped breathing, for Ladywater showed Thomas to me.

Just his face at first. His true-blue eyes gazing into mine, a plea in them, and love and grief and pain that pierced my heart like a dagger. Around the edges of the pain, part of my mind noticed that he wore a soft hat of wine-colored velvet, not a warrior's helm. And a velvet cape, and—where was he? What was happening to him? I saw that he was on his knees, supplicating, his hands lifting toward me, and—the misery in his eyes—

Such misery that I could not bear to see. I blinked, shook my head and looked away.

What could this be? I sensed quite surely that Thomas was riding toward me. Very near now.

But—Ladywater did not lie.

And Ladywater was kind.

What was it that I had seen? And *when* was it?

I drew a long breath and looked at the pool again, but now I saw only the shining surface of the water showing me images of reeds, blossoms, sky, clouds.

I did not really wish to see anything more. What fearsome thing had I scried?

Frowning, I stood up, looking around me—and what I saw sent all thought of the vision fleeing from my mind.

Over the top of the hill a knight came riding. At first I saw only his helmed head, bent, but even then I knew him and began to run toward him.

A knight riding a weary horse, a battered knight with one arm in a sling, his shield hanging from his saddle. Its device, a single heart-shaped green leaf with a violet blossom.

As I ran toward him he lifted his head, and his eyes smiled at me the warmest blue the world has ever known.

16

Lying at his ease on a couch in the sunshine, with his head pillowed on cushions scented with rosemary, his hair strewn in shining black curls across the white linen, Thomas smiled up at me. "My sweet lady," he murmured. "You terrify me."

"How so?" Although he smiled, his words astonished me. Sitting on a broidery chair to keep him company, in my simplest green gown with my hair in plaits down my shoulders, I could not imagine what had put such a thought into his mind.

He said, faltering a little, for he was still very weak, "You—you commanded me here—"

The summons. He had ridden through rivers of blood to get here. I had not considered, when I sent for him, I had not remembered how the force of such a sending would allow no rest. He had barely slept on his way here. And when combatants had come in his way he had not made shift to avoid them, but had fought his way through, riding on when he was wounded, riding on when he was almost too weak and worn to stand.

"I had forgotten what it was like to be summoned," I told him humbly. "I am sorry, Thomas. If I had thought, I would have made shift to do it more gently." The way I had healed him. I had learned, finally, how to use my milpreve with mindful caution, so that we were partners in magic, the druid stone and I, and I could somewhat govern it not to hurt me. I had made shift in that way to heal the worst of Thomas's wounds without wounding myself, letting time take care of the rest: the bad memories, the bone-deep weariness.

"It was as if you pulled me here by an invisible line and a hook caught in my heart." Thomas gazed into my eyes, all in wonder, not bitter at all. "Such power—it unmans me."

"More than the clashing power of knights in battle?"

"Yes. No." I sensed in him a memory, quickly suppressed, of his father captured, his own capture when he was but a boy. "I don't know. That power I have known all my life. But this—it's uncanny."

"It is uncanny that I should wish you by me?"

He caught my teasing tone and smiled anew. "Yes. I cannot encompass it. You did—all this—"

His glance and a movement of his hand took it all in: Caer Morgana. The many candles and pleasant gold-groined chambers drawn from my memories of Avalon, the courtyard where we were enjoying a day of sunshine, the arbors of fruit trees, the white doves nesting in the ivy, the blue roses blooming.

"Do you not like it?" I teased.

"I—it is paradise." He stirred as if some bad dream troubled him, shifting his head on the pillows. He whispered, "But—such power—"

"Shhhh." He had seen too many horrors if he saw something fearsome in me, I decided. "Hush, Thomas. Just rest. Or are you hungry? Thirsty?"

"Maybe—something to drink—"

I touched my milpreve, sent a thought, and in a moment one of the servants, I think it was Gilly, hurried out with a goblet of pear ambrosia on a tray. I smiled, for goblet and tray were of matching silver beaded with gold. Gilly was learning.

Thomas watched as she placed the tray on a little table at his right side. She should have handed him the goblet also, but she went away without doing so. I would speak to her later.

Thomas turned his blue gaze back to me. Like a puzzled child he said, "I miss the piskies and their mischief."

"Do you truly?" I did not. I preferred to have my stockings mended and my meals prepared without mischief, thank you; I had never liked hearing the little wretches giggling behind my back in the evenings. I preferred them obedient, as they were now. Still, if Thomas missed them . . . "If you want mischief," I said slowly, "I suppose we could manage some. When you're stronger."

"My lady . . ." Thomas shook his head with a look I could not quite understand, as if he wanted to laugh or cry.

"What, Thomas?"

"Nothing. I was thinking that mischief is not mischief if it is managed, that is all." He reached for his goblet of pear ambrosia, lifted it toward me and asked, "Would you not like some also, my lady?"

I shook my head with a smile. I smiled often those days; it was heavenly to have him there with me, my faithful knight, my True Thomas.

He drank, set the goblet upon its tray, then asked me, "Do you never thirst, Lady Morgan?"

"Of course I do." Silly boy. "But I go down to the pool and drink at the spring."

He gave me an oddly intent gaze. "Still? Like when you were a child here?"

"Yes."

"But, my lady, why do you not ask a servant to bring you springwater if it is springwater you crave?"

"I . . ." But I loved the pool. I always sat for at least a few minutes there, alone with the herons and rushes and the mirroring water. This morning I had watched the dawn brighten that water and turn it blue—rare, such blue water, such a blue-sky day, by this stormy, misty seaside. I had watched the pool shine as blue as Thomas's eyes.

Why not ask a servant to bring me springwater? Something in Thomas's question and his sky blue gaze tested me, and I did not like that. Therefore I did not tell him the truth, or not the whole truth.

"The servants are for you," I said.

"But if I would rather walk down to the pool and drink at the spring?"

"Then of course you should do so, Thomas," I said. "When you are well again. Hush, now, and rest."

"You rest in the grass and violets, do you not, my lady?" Thomas asked softly. "You rest awhile and gaze at the peaceful water?"

"Shhh, Thomas! Save talking for when you are feeling stronger."

We would have a lifetime for talking.

He smiled at me, obeyed me and closed his blue, blue eyes.

I had not yet given him the ring that I had made for him. My token. A knight must earn the token of his lady, and Thomas had not yet had a chance to do so. But he would; I felt certain he would.

"I could give you a mare just like Annie," I told Thomas.

"No, my lady, please." He rode the tall saddle horse I had magicked for him, shining black to match his hair—it is not hard to make a horse given a stick of blackthorn or two and the right dreams to work with, and Thomas often dreamed of horses, sleek prancing horses, usually black or dapple-gray but once in a while sunny gold. I rode the golden gelding at his side; with the summer wind lifting our hair like wings we rode the crest of the moor, and although Thomas did not know it, the walls of Caer Morgana followed along with us, invisible fortifications encircling us to protect us. Thomas would meet with no knights errant upon this summer day.

My stables were like my battlements, invisible and without set form or size, taking no space at all, yet in them I kept any steed Thomas or I could wish to ride, whether a swan-necked red or silver mare of the hot Araby blood, a black charger, or a gentle white palfrey. And, yes, a dapple-gray mare just like Annie, only larger.

"It would break my heart," Thomas said.

I nodded. That was why I had not showed her to him.

Something in the face of the moor that day reminded me of

Rhiannon, all flowers and flutter, heather as green as her wise merry eyes, white and yellow butterflies flitting to sip at bluestars, buttercups, heartsease, daisies.

"Sir Thomas," I said, trying hard to be more formal than coy, "I wish you to bring me a bouquet of butterflies." I could not keep a smile from tugging at the corners of my mouth, confound it.

He looked at me with astonishment quirking his eyebrows, laughter hiding in his blue eyes, a dawning of color in the pearl white skin over his cheekbones, his mouth severely grave. "My lady's wish is my command," he declared, swinging his leg over his saddle to leap down off his horse. Thanks to my care and his own strength and goodness of heart, he was as well and strong as ever.

"And make sure you don't hurt any of them," I added.

He gave me a look that made me duck my head to keep from laughing. This solemn silliness, that a knight must perform the tasks his lady commanded of him whether possible or not, earned him her favor and her token. When I looked up, Thomas was darting toward a patch of daisies aflutter with butterflies, his blue velvet cape flying over his linen shirt as if he himself had wings.

I watched, thinking of the more serious quest he had already performed for me: finding my half brother, Arthur. A stripling named Arthur, he had told me, lived with the family of one Sir Ector of the north midlands, nobly reared but of no known parentage. Meanwhile, all the petty kings and pretenders churned the land with their wars, Lothe of Lothian marching on Uryens of Gore, while Gore besieged Caer Argent to take it from Redburke or Carados or whoever occupied it at the time, unless it was Caer Leon they were fighting over today; it went on and on, relentless. Never ending.

Never to take my Thomas away.

Thomas's horse slowly strayed, grazing despite the bit in its mouth and the reins falling around its ears. Soon it would step on the reins and either spook itself or break them or both. As a proper haughty lady, I should have let the horse do what it would and enjoyed watching Thomas deal with the annoyance. But as Morgan, I found that I could torment Thomas only just so much. I rolled my eyes, rode after the straying horse, dismounted and stood in the furze holding both horses by the reins. I was trying to think how to tether them so as not to look like a servant lass when, confound everything, Thomas walked up behind me.

I heard his footsteps and turned. "Lady Morgan," he said with just a hint, a ripple, of laughter marring the smooth surface of the words. He bowed low, presenting me with an armful of blossoms—daisies, buttercups, bluestars. Beautiful.

"But Sir Thomas, they are not butterflies," I said, finding it very hard to keep a petulant face and chide.

"The butterflies will follow, my lady," he said, and even as he spoke, one floated down a shaft of sunshine and lit on the topmost blossom, fanning wings all jewel colors, topaz and ruby and amethyst, more exquisite than my mother's finest jewels.

Mother. Forever crying and scrying for Arthur, Arthur. Now that I knew, or thought I knew, where Arthur was, did I mean to tell her?

No. No, I wanted only to abide at Caer Morgana with Thomas.

"My lady, will you not be seated?" he asked, smiling, taking the reins of the two horses from me. "The turf is as soft as a couch of green velvet. Prithee, sit awhile. May I make for you a crown?"

With a regal nod I deigned to seat myself. The jewel-colored butterfly had flitted away, but sunbeams warmed me like love, and I held my wildflower bouquet like a baby in my arms, thinking, I don't know why, of the blossom girl in the old story Morgause had read to Ongwynn and me one night. I watched Thomas lead the horses to a distance and hobble them, then start plucking daisies and weaving the stems together. I wondered whether he would add other flowers to my crown. I wondered whether he had ever plucked the petals of a daisy, whispering *she loves me, she loves me not*, whether he had been thinking of me. Another butterfly, garnet and lapis this time, floated down to land on one of the starflowers in my arms.

Whispering a small wish, I hugged my flowers and fingered my milpreve. In a moment, butterflies drifted out of the sky like golden and crimson and blue leaves falling, like great bright snowflakes. They alighted by the dozen on the blossoms in my arms, butterflies upon every bloom, every petal, cloud sea mist white amethyst sunshine sapphire porphyry and pearl, butterflies crowding butterflies until they could scarcely fan their heavenly wings.

I cried, "Thomas, look!"

He turned, and his eyes widened, for in my embrace I held a bouquet of butterflies.

17

THAT WAS THE DAY I MOST REMEMBER, NOW THAT I FLY over battlefields and the screams of dying men echo up to me as fate falls like soot from my gray wings. I think back upon many sweet mortal days, but that day of wildflowers and butterflies, that was the sweetest.

There were other such days, heavenly days. Thomas grew strong and well and served my small demands ardently, and I gave my token to him, the ring woven of my hair. By that token my knight, True Thomas, knew that I cherished him. And by his deeds I knew that he adored me. All was as it should be.

Or so I thought.

Fate thought otherwise.

It started small, as such dooms often do. It began because sometimes I needed to be by myself, away from the questions of the servants and, yes, away from Thomas's adoration, away from my own love for him, love so ardent and hungry it frightened me and I never dared to show it to him entirely. Just as I had stolen away sometimes to be alone in my quoit stone when I was a child, sometimes I stole away to be alone by the pool or, this time, by the sea.

The tide ran high, answering the call of the moon at her strongest, and I sat just above the wet grit with my skirts in a muddle like the wrack at the edge of the waves, with my fingers sorting shells and pebbles for no reason, with nothing in my mind but pink cream amber, when footfalls crunched toward me, running. I looked up.

"Thomas?"

"My lady." He plunged to his knees in the gravel beside me, panting. "My—Morgan, I wanted to walk out on the moor, and something would not let me. It was—it was like a wall of air."

"Yes," I said, looking back at him stupidly I suppose, for I did not yet understand why he had become so distraught.

He demanded, "Did you do that?"

"Yes."

"But why?"

"I didn't want a visible wall," I said, lifting my grubby hands full of pebbles and whelks, explaining as best I could. "I wanted to be able to see the sea." Most castle walls were ugly, cutting off light and air.

Sitting on his heels, Thomas stared at me, his face on a level with mine, his blue eyes clouded with a trouble I did not understand.

Belatedly I realized that Thomas had not realized that there were walls at all. As they had been composed so as to let him in, and as they went along when I rode out with him, how was he to know? I never should have left him to roam Caer Morgana on his own. "This is a castle," I explained. "The walls are to stop intruders." Other than him. A few times my sentries had reported riders to me, knights errant, scouts. The walls had stopped them out of sight of my domed dwelling, my courtyard and fruit trees and Ladywater pool, my blue roses.

"But, my lady," Thomas asked me quietly, "how am I to get out?"

"Just come to me," I said.

The trouble in his eyes deepened. He did not speak.

I tried to explain. "It is like any castle. Someone must open the gate, that is all." I looked down at my hands and saw how dirty they were. Dropping stones and bits of broken shell, I rose to my feet and stooped as the reaching tip of a wave ran up to me, washing my fingers in the salt water. Thomas stayed where he was.

"Do you still wish to go walking on the moor?" I asked him. "I will come with you."

He shook his head. "I no longer wish to go."

After that day, I no longer stole away to the sea to be by myself. I ventured no farther than the spring pool, from where I would see Thomas if he walked outside.

I did not yet know myself to be a liar. He knew it, I think, sooner than I.

Truth was, I could have composed the walls to let Thomas out whenever he desired it, just as I had composed them to let him in.

Just come to me, I had said, as if it were nothing, only a matter of my being the lady of Caer Morgana, the one who had to give certain orders.

I did not know myself to be a liar until some days later, when Thomas tested my word.

Shadowed days. Thomas devoted himself to me as a knight and courtier should, but in the nights, sitting in the courtyard as I often did in company with the stars and moon, I sensed that his dreams were troubled. And the same trouble, the same fear, hid gray in the blue of his eyes during those days, and my smile could not cozen it away.

Sometimes his attention wandered and he stared at nothing, stared away. "Sir Thomas," I chided that day I should have kept silence, "you are distracted."

"Yes," he said quietly. "I am." It was a misty gray day; even I, Morgan le Fay, could not make the sky be always sunny for Thomas and me. We sat in the solarium looking out over the sea, watching the waves break their white spines on the rocks, watching young gannets try their wings. Soon the snow geese would make vees in the sky. Soon it would be autumn, then winter, cozy for some, dark and lonely for others. As I thought this, Thomas gave me a sideward look worthy of Ongwynn, as blank as stone. "My lady, I would like to ride along the sea."

On such a gray day, threatening rain? But I said, "The sea air would do me good. I will come with you."

Thomas stood, but did not offer me his hand. "Thank you, my lady, but no, I would like to go alone. Will you open the gates for me? And," he added with a wry smile, "tell me where they are?"

Terror too deep to understand gripped my heart like a giant's gauntleted fist. "No!" I blurted before I could think. At once I tried to soften the word. "I mean, not today."

"Not today? Why?"

"My sentries tell me there are riders skulking about. Some lord's vanguard, perhaps, scouting." This was true, though it was news of no importance to me except as my excuse to keep Thomas by my side.

"Invisible sentries? Do they know whose men-at-arms those might be?"

"No." Rooks were smart as birds go, smarter even than crows, and like crows they made marvelous sentries, ever vigilant, and they could speak to me. But Thomas had just bespoken their limit. "No, they cannot say." Devices on shields meant nothing to them.

Thomas stood lance straight. "Then all the more reason, my lady, that I should ride forth to see who threatens you."

The steely grip of fear on my heart tightened. *No. Please.* My father had ridden forth never to return. I could not let Thomas leave me. I could not.

"There is no threat," I said between dry lips, and although I would have lied to keep him by me, I believed I spoke the truth, and I spoke strongly.

Uncertain now, Thomas gazed at me without speaking.

I rose to stand facing him and spoke to him for once as Morgan, his longtime friend. "Thomas, it would be folly to court danger for no reason. Stay here. Please."

He gave me a doubtful glance, then a nod and a bow. In silence he sat again, and I sat beside him, and in silence we watched the sea.

I hoped that was the end of it. But although Thomas gave me his smile the next morning, the shadow had deepened in his eyes.

I did my best, the few days that followed, to divert him. Although I knew my fey powers gave him pause, I used them to summon into the courtyard singing birds, linnets and larks and nightingales to lighten his heart. I gifted him with a pure white fawn to be his pet. I whimmed rainbow fountains out of the sea. I magicked a juggler to shorten one long evening, and tumblers such as I remembered from Arthur's name-day long ago at Avalon, and a jester to make us laugh. The last evening—although I did not know it was the last evening—I magicked a minstrel who played upon his harp more sweetly than the chiming of bluebells, who sang like golden honey flowing. Because I had made him, he sang my thoughts, and therefore he sang no ballads of knightly deeds or courage in warfare; rather, he sang songs of love.

> *My lady love is a fair white candle*
> *Who scorches my heart with her flame;*
> *My lady love is sweet winged fire*
> *No man can hope to tame.*
> *I have given my heart to my lady fair*
> *And my love has made me her prisoner . . .*

I felt my heart go watery and stole a look at Thomas, but he did not answer my glance, and even in the firelight I could see how his eyes had saddened and the softness of his mouth had gone hard.

My Thomas.

The honeyed singing of the minstrel might as well have been the barking of a crow to me now.

I slept badly that night, and left my bed at dawn. In the chill of early morning I sat by the spring pool and gazed long into its still waters, trying to find something of peace or hope there. But all was dismal fog gray, all around me and all within my mind. Ladywater had nothing to say to me that day.

Thomas rose early also. I found him sitting idly in the courtyard when I entered. He wore a cape and hat of soft wine-colored velvet—the servants supplied him with the most lovely clothes, in accordance with my dreams. I stood just looking at him, he was so beautiful.

"My lady." He rose and bowed over the hand I offered, the hand that wore a ring made of his hair. He touched my hand with his, ring to ring. I loved that touch. But he had not yet dared to kiss my hand.

My gentle Thomas.

I sat down, and he sat by my side. Servants came and brought us fresh toasted honey scones and milk and roasted apples for breakfast. We ate, the fog lifted and turned to rainbow in the misty sunshine, nightingales sang from the ivy—but Thomas seemed neither to hear the birds' sweet singing nor taste the sweet food, and I ate little.

"Roasted apples," I said to break the silence. "Bah. How common." Lightly, mocking myself, trying to make him smile with my ladylike nonsense. "Sir Thomas, what I should really like is a bowl of wild strawberries in cream." The season for wild strawberries had passed a month before.

"Your wish is my command, my lady," Thomas murmured, but he did not smile. He merely stood to go find something to try to please me. No chuckle, no quizzical lift to his eyebrows, no—

He turned back. "No," he said too loudly for courtesy.

I felt the steel grip of terror. I could not speak.

"No," Thomas said more quietly, "no more of this game. My lady, I cannot live this way."

I could barely stir my dry lips to whisper, "Thomas, what—what is wrong?"

"I am not a man any longer; I am your toy. I am shackled in your pretty dungeon. I cannot bear it." He turned and strode out.

Sentries winged in to report to me, their presence urgent in the air, but I brushed them aside; I lunged up and ran after Thomas.

He had covered half the distance to the walls before I caught up to him amid pomegranate trees. "Thomas," I cried, panting, "where would you go?"

"Anywhere." He turned to face me, and I felt the full force of the storm gray misery in his eyes. "My lady, I am of no purpose, no use here—"

"But—I—"

"It is not your fault, my lady," Thomas said. "I am to blame if I cannot be content with pleasing you."

"—I can find a way—"

"No."

"Thomas, let me try—"

"No. Give me some worthy quest, my lady. I could take news of your brother to your mother at Avalon—"

"No!" I cried. No, dear lady mother of us all, no, he wanted to ride away into danger and leave me and I might never see him again.

Something in my face or my cry made him stare at me, then turn and stride away again.

My chest had gone tight with trying not to weep and I could

not run after him anymore, not with the heavy silk gown beating around my legs, the thin useless slippers falling off my feet, and even though I knew the walls would not let him pass, I could not bear to see him storm away from me. I whimpered, "Thomas, come back," and touched my milpreve. The ring made of his hair would have served as well and would have been gentler, but I was not thinking.

In a moment Thomas came back into view between the trees, walking toward me yet leaning back as if rough hands dragged and shoved him along, and the horror on his face stabbed me like a dagger to the heart, yet I could not admit that I, I who loved him, was hurting him. And I was terrified because he wanted to leave me, and therefore I did not take away my touch from my druid-power ring until he toppled forward as if he had been flung my way, fell to his knees before me and bowed his head.

"My lady, please," he said softly.

"Sir Thomas, you need not kneel. Stand," I said, all lady kindness.

He did not stand. He flung back his head, glared into my eyes and cried, "My Lady Morgan, for the love of all mercy, let me go!" His hands lifted toward me, supplicant.

Thomas. My Thomas, his true-blue eyes gazing into mine, the agony in them pitiful. Dear Thomas, on his knees to me, pleading. And his pain smote me to the heart of my heart, and I saw: Mother of misery, I had done this to him.

Cernunnos had tried to warn me. I was not whole, not ready, he had said.

Ongwynn had tried to warn me.

All powers above and below, even the sweet lady mother of

us all, had tried. This moment was the one that Ladywater had tried to show me.

In that moment, as Thomas cried out to me like a criminal condemned to die and my own wretched heart cried out against me, I knew: If I were not to hate myself forevermore, I had to let him go.

Yet I whispered, "I cannot."

"My lady, I am begging you! I cannot be a prisoner, not even of love; I cannot bear it!"

My love had made him prisoner, not his own. I had to let him go.

Yet truly I could not.

Deep, deep as I searched myself, I could not find freedom for Thomas in me.

His hands trembling, his voice trembling, Thomas pleaded, "Morgan, think back. That first day, when I was just a stripling and you were a grubby-nosed little girl—"

Tears I had held back for days stung their way out of my eyes. Weeping like a child, I folded to my knees facing Thomas, my own supplication the equal of his. I sobbed, "I can't do it."

He tore off his velvet hat and flung it away hard, as if it had done all this trouble to him. But his voice remained soft as he said, "Morgan, of course you can."

I shook my head and faced him as if facing a king's judgment. Facing him, crying, I told him, "Thomas, I can . . . converse with finches and . . . and fallow deer . . . I can summon butterflies . . . turn stone into gold . . . make a paradise for you, bring forth roses out of . . . deep winter snow, but I . . . I cannot let you go."

"You must."

"I cannot! I do not have such power."

Silence.

In deep silence Thomas faced me, his gaze quieting like his breathing as he began to comprehend. Truly I think he understood, for he gently gathered my hands into his. Kneeling, we faced each other, I looked into his eyes and, oh, goddess of wonders, all powers be praised, I saw love there. Even though he knew me now, knew me to my dark, needy and greedy heart, still—Oh, my Thomas, still he loved me, his love so warm and vast I could barely encompass it, or comprehend his forgiveness of me.

And I wept all the harder with relief, because I thought all would be well now.

"Morgan," he murmured, "you have held my heart in your hands since that very first day."

I could not speak.

He stood, keeping my hands in his, lifting me to my feet. "Morgan, I shall always love you," he whispered, and he kissed me.

Never before had he kissed me, not even on the hand.

Never before had any man kissed me that way.

He kissed me softly on the lips, and that feathery warm touch stopped my heart then set it to pounding, lidded my eyes, made me gasp and sway on my feet. I knew nothing, I could think nothing, there was nothing but Thomas, Thomas, all time all love all living dying yearning in the touch of his mouth to mine—

And as he kissed me so tenderly, without my noticing he ever so gently slipped the milpreve ring off my finger.

With a crackling roar like that of a great fire, the orchard of pomegranate trees burst into splinters and fell to the ground around us.

My eyes snapped open, but nothing made sense. Fruit trees falling to dust, the golden dome of Caer Morgana shattering and falling into shards of dusky-green seawater, and amid the froth the screeches of—of piskies, and the courtyard gone, the blue roses gone, and so much noise, rooks flying over with harsh cries, many men shouting and cheering, steely clamor of shields and swords, an army of hooves pounding toward me at the gallop, my own pulse pounding in my ears, Thomas exclaiming, "Morgan, I'm sorry!"

Thomas, standing at arm's length from me, the milpreve in his hands, his perfect face as white and shadowed as the moon.

Too near at hand, amid the dust of many knights, I glimpsed the face of one of them, a helmed rider charging upon us both, a surly turnip-nosed face, a dangerous face all too familiar yet utterly strange and wrong in what should have been Caer Morgana.

Redburke.

Grinning because he saw me, he knew me.

Raising his broadsword.

Thomas whirled to face Redburke, dropping the milpreve. Without any weapon he sprang to place himself between death and me.

Redburke struck as if swatting a fly. His first blow sliced off Thomas's hand, lifted as if to raise a shield—but there was no shield. Redburke's second blow took off Thomas's head.

In the moment it took me to snatch up the milpreve from the ground, Thomas fell dead.

I saw—I can barely speak of it, even now. Slantwise as I stood up I saw . . . his severed head falling.

I felt my heart splinter like the pomegranate trees.

Redburke loomed over me. With no thought for self or caution I screamed, "Death! Death to all of you!" The milpreve blazed so furious it blinded me; I saw only white fire. Then I slammed into the ground, and everything went black for a merciful while.

18

I REMEMBER HEARING THE CROAKING OF RAVENS, BUT not understanding. I blinked up at a swirl of black wings against a twilight sky. I remember feeling several kinds of racking pain, in my hand, my body, my heart, but not knowing why. Then I sat up and saw.

Ravens picking out my father's eyes.

Rather, at first in my muddled mind I thought it was my father. I saw a battlefield. Bodies and carrion birds everywhere. Feasting upon—no, it was not my father. It was Redburke.

And nearby—Thomas.

His dead, bloody, severed head, its empty eye sockets turned toward me.

Already my heart had splintered to bits. In that moment my mind did the same. I felt it shatter.

I went mad.

• • •

Like my mother, I went mad.

The difference being, she had run crazed because of what had been done to her. But I ran crazed because of what I had done.

She had loved my father, and her love for him had made her soft and weak, so Ongwynn had said.

I had loved Thomas. What had loving him done to me?

I ran mad.

My memories of that time are bits and pieces I must search for amid the madness, like shards of broken shell amid the black grit of the seashore.

I remember seeing piskies—the little brown brats climbed upon me as I curled amid heather on the moor, pouring water on my face, forcing bread into my mouth. At the time it seemed to me that they were tormenting me and I deserved it, but I think now that they were trying to help, and to this day I cannot encompass such mercy after what I had done to them.

I remember hearing voices in the wind—Daddy, Cernunnos, Rhiannon, Thomas, Morgause, Mother, Ongwynn. Mostly they reproached me; only Ongwynn tried to comfort me. I remember looking for Ongwynn—I thought I was a child, and with my hair tangled like a moor pony's mane, with dirt and tears crusted on my face, I ran into Caer Ongwynn. Unless the madness deludes me, it was a hollow hill again, a rude stone haven, all just as it used to be, but no one was there, Ongwynn was not there, and I wept and stamped my feet and stormed off to find her.

I must have strayed far, for I remember a village woman throwing something at me from a safe distance—stones, I thought. I snatched one up left-handed to hurl it back at her, and saw that it was bread, and gnawed at it while I glared at her from under the hair hanging in my eyes.

I remember my own crippled right hand, with an odd sort of blue stone embedded amid melted metal in the seared flesh of the palm. I did not even recognize my own milpreve. My crazed mind would not let me think what it was, what had happened, how my hand had gotten that way.

I remember cows gazing down at me as I awoke from sleeping in their hay. I remember how the steam rose from the warm bulk of their bodies in a frosty autumn dawn. I remember them because their white breath warmed me. But I did not want to be warm. I wanted to be cold, because cold numbed my pain.

I remember lying in snow, and wondering how it was that white snow could look black at night, and welcoming the bone-deep chill, not caring whether I died.

I think it might have been that night that Cernunnos found me, just as he had once found my mother crouching as wild as a hare amid the heather.

Avalon. Wellspring of womanhood, wellspring of Lady-water, place of peril, place of healing.

I do not remember being carried home to Avalon in Cernunnos's arms—that was told to me later. I remember first the scent of violets—it was spring already when I awakened to find myself lying pillowed amid gauzy white linen in a bower by the waterside. Years later, when they took him there, King Arthur might have awakened in much the same way, bowered in flower-scented fleecy softness with the lady of Avalon by his side.

Rhiannon smiled down at me, her green eyes merry and sad and not a day older than when I had seen her last.

"Do you know me, Morgan?" she asked.

"Of course I know you!" I struggled to sit up, surprised to find myself thin and weak under a gown of creamy lambswool. "Rhiannon—what has happened? What am I doing here?"

To my surprise, her bright eyes misted. I had never seen such emotion in her before. She had to look away from me. "Later," she said. "Eat first."

But as I hoisted myself, I felt an odd lump in my right hand, and I looked. "My milpreve," I whispered, bewildered, and then in my partly healed heart I felt a shadow, a distant intimation, of the rage and pain with which I had felled Redburke's army, and I remembered.

Thomas.

Oh, my love.

I remembered everything, and I cried out to Avalon, "I cannot bear it!" and flung myself facedown on the white bed and wept.

I felt as if I would die. In a sense it was true that I could not bear what had happened. It had driven me mad, and it had taken all the healers of Avalon to bring me back. If it had not been for the ring on Rhiannon's finger and the gentling touch of her hands on my shoulders, I might have gone mad again.

Many days passed, I do not know how many, before I could bear to speak to Rhiannon, or to any of the friends who attended me. And seasons passed before I could bear to tell them of Thomas's death.

Seasons passed on tiptoe in Avalon, as I have said. I remember a violet-scented day when I sat in the arbor and watched the wee ducks swimming and I talked with Cernunnos—it seems like the same year, but I think it was a year later.

It must have been, for I had scried by then that Morgause was safe; she had married King Lothe of Lothian. And I knew that my mother still spent her days sitting in darkness under the dome of Avalon, her haunted eyes gazing into a shadowed mirror, begging, "Arthur. Show me Arthur. I want my son."

Arthur! How I detested the name. Why should he have a mother who loved him when I, Morgan, daughter of the same mother, had no one?

Still, I somewhat understood now how she had come to be the way she was. My heart still ached with longing for Thomas.

Cernunnos and I sat under the shade of the same arbor where Thomas had rested in soft greensward, where I had knighted him and had given him a useless quest to send him out of danger into what had seemed like lesser danger at the time. The memory seemed to come to me from a lifetime ago.

The tiny jewel-bright ducks swam in a pool like a sky blue mirror, and in the water their reflections showed as the wings of butterflies, sapphire, topaz, ruby, amethyst.

That urging from Ladywater helped me speak. "Thomas once gathered for me a bouquet of butterflies," I told Cernunnos.

With his gleaming antler tips almost touching the arbor leaves, he lounged in the grass, turning his fey golden eyes my way. "No one could have loved him better than you did," he said.

"I killed him." The three words might as well have been three daggers stabbing my heart.

Cernunnos eyed me, his golden gaze unreadable. "As I recall," he said mildly, "you told me Redburke killed him."

"Yes," I said, my throat tightening against grief, "but if it had not been for my folly—"

"Your only folly was to try to cheat fate."

"I tried to imprison him. Now he's dead."

Cernunnos shook his head, his antlers rattling against the arbor posts. "Morgan, use your good, strong mind. Think. You were only trying to save Thomas. And what would have happened to him if you had not tried?"

"I—I don't know. He might be alive now."

"No. I think not. His span of life was determined when he was born. You know he was fated to die in battle."

"But—"

"When you tried to defy fate, you took fate's third strand in your hands."

As Ongwynn had tried to warn me not to. As was written in the book of threes; was I the thorny-hearted maid, or the blackwing Morrigun after all? I could hardly bear to think of what fate had done to make me be fate, of what I had done. "Please," I whispered.

Cernunnos stirred his brown-furred shoulders impatiently. "Morgan, he knew. The first night he sheltered here, he saw the Morrigun washing his bloody corpse. He saw me and my hounds hunting his soul across the sky."

My aching heart stopped beating for a moment, and I felt an awesome silence in which there was nothing, no pain, no power, no struggle, no comprehension. I gawked at Cernunnos.

"But he was wiser than you," Cernunnos added more quietly, "and he accepted, and lived out his allotted span."

I barely managed to speak. "You did not really—set the hounds on his soul, when he died—"

"No. No, I took him in my arms."

I breathed again.

Cernunnos said, "Truly, Morgan, it is no wonder that you grieve so for him. He was such a one as this wretched world has seldom known."

I would not have believed it a moment before, but yes, I heard sorrow in his voice, saw sorrow in his eyes. My heart came alive again, warmed by his words.

"I will tell you a tale of fate," Cernunnos said, but I shook my head, stood up, thanked him with the best smile I could muster, and left him, walking barefoot in the spring grass down to the pool where the white swans floated, their reflections shining like ebony.

After that day, though, I carried a sense of fate in the closed fist of my mind, and remembered one by one, in time, the tales of fate I had heard, and in time I opened my mind a little and allowed Cernunnos to tell me more. But it was Rhiannon who told me the tale that I remember most often to this day, and it is this: There was once a knight whose liege king had gifted him with a golden goblet, a great heavy vessel fit for a prince. But when his lady saw the goblet, she turned white as a swan. Throw it in the sea, she said. It is your death. But the knight would not give up his kingly gift. So as he slept, his lady stole the goblet and hid it until she could think how to destroy it. When the knight awoke and found his goblet gone, he was enraged. What have you done with it? he roared at his lady. And when she would not answer, he struck her so hard that she stumbled and fell against a doorway. And the goblet, which she had placed in a high niche above the doorway, fell down upon the knight's head, killing him.

Like me, the lady had tried to save her beloved.

It still hurt like fire to think of Thomas's death, but in a slantwise way all that had happened started to make sense to me.

There came a summer day—it might have been a month or more than a year after I had talked with Cernunnos—a floating water-lily day when I swam naked with Rhiannon and many others in a pool of Ladywater as warm as a womb, and the minnows nibbled at my belly and my toes, and all was peace for a while.

Then everything changed, not only for me but for all who dwelt in Avalon, never to be the same.

There was no warning. All in a moment the earth quaked, sending the minnows darting for the shallows. With a clamor the mound of Avalon blossomed open—it should never have done so under the sun, never until twilight. Then, as we scrambled to the shore and stood bare and staring, out from under a gilded archway, out of a grassy portal, a scrawny figure staggered, then stood blinking in the bright summer light.

I did not at first recognize her, for in many, many years I had not seen her in the sunshine.

She shaded her eyes from the day's glory with both brittle hands. She peered straight at me but past me. "My son!" she cried to all of us. "Arthur has drawn the sword from the stone." Sword? Stone? The words made no sense to any of us, but Mother seemed to know what they meant. "My son!" she cried to the blue sky. "My son, they will crown him King!"

19

Bᴜᴛ ʜᴏᴡ ᴡɪʟʟ ʏᴏᴜ ɢᴏ?" ɪ ᴀsᴋᴇᴅ ᴍʏ ᴍᴏᴛʜᴇʀ. Mᴀɴʏ
others had asked her the same question.

Busy sorting through a shimmering pile of gowns mounded
on her bed, trying to decide what to wear to the coronation,
she answered me just as she had answered them. "You will
see." Distracted, cheerful, smiling. "I am sent for. Arthur
knows who his mother is now, and he wants to meet me." And
truly he would meet his mother, Igraine the Beautiful, for despite the lines of age she was beautiful again, color in her
cheeks now, her hair sleek, and even a little flesh beginning to
soften her thin body. Somehow Arthur had cured her when I
could not.

Arthur. My half brother, a fifteen-year-old stripling who
would be King while Thomas lay dead. Why should this un-
tried youth, this Arthur, my half brother, have a throne when
I, who knew much and had suffered much, had nothing? I had
not met Arthur since his name-day, when he had lain a fat

baby in my mother's arms, but sitting on a hard chair in my mother's chamber I still despised him every bit as much as I had then, with the fire dragon burning in my heart and vengeful thoughts blazing in my mind. Thinking of him, wishing him ill, I felt the milpreve go hot in its metal nest in the palm of my hand.

My mother sighed over the gowns the fays were offering her. "I shall look so odd," she murmured. "No jewels . . . but I suppose fashions have changed. Do you know?" She turned and smiled at me, cordial.

"No."

"You have not been out either for a long time?"

"No. I haven't."

"Oh, well, perhaps my son Arthur will give me some jewels. Rubies would be nice. I used to have the most lovely rubies. I wonder what has become of them—"

"Mother?" I interrupted her prattling.

She looked at me blankly. Half the time I felt not at all sure she knew who I was.

"I used to have a ring made of your hair," I told her, "but it wore out. Would you make me another one before you leave?"

"Oh? Oh, certainly, dear, when I have time. But I have so much to do. Arthur's coronation—"

I got up and wandered out of her chamber, soothing the milpreve with a fingertip. Mother had probably forgotten my request already. And the ring Thomas had given me was gone, I did not know how, probably burned right off my hand on that awful day, so that I did not have even that small circle of shining black hair to remember him by. My hands bore no ornament except the milpreve in its nest of melted orichalcum, bedded to the bone in my palm. Never before, I thought, had a lady worn a stone so strangely.

The milpreve and I both wanted to do something spiteful, but I did not yet know what. I avoided my mother during the days that followed, but I heard that she was busy embroidering a headdress for herself.

"Am I to send her off as I did you, alone on a dead knight's charger?" Cernunnos asked me, brows raised.

"I don't know."

No one knew. And Avalon stood open night and day, and no one knew the why or how of that either. There was worried talk, then a waiting silence. Nothing untoward had yet happened, but I could feel the waiting, a silence of waiting like the silence of a heron standing in the shallows. Even the little ducks had gone silent, and even the breezes held their breath, even the windflowers stood still, waiting, and the ripples stilled in the pools and streams.

My mother finished her embroidery, I surmise, for one morning as I walked past the arbor to bathe my face in the swan pool, she issued forth with her headdress in place, mantled and gowned for a journey. The friends who had sheltered her for these many years followed her like servants, carrying her bags. All of Avalon came out to watch—something, who knew what? Igraine the Beautiful clearly and serenely expected to depart. She stood smiling before the sunny portal.

I saw this, then turned my back, sitting on the grassy verge of the swan pool and gazing at myself in the mirroring water.

The pudgy, powdered face of middle-aged Morgan smirked back at me, her hard eyes glinting with a mirth I did not like or understand.

She horrified me. But I sat silent just to see what might happen next. The fire dragon?

No. Not this time. Instead, the face turned to that of a sooty black bird, so large and near that I could see the membranes at the corners of its yellow eyes, the bony nostrils piercing its beak hard and sharp and heavy as a broadsword.

And the blue stone blazing, imbedded in its feathered forehead much as it now nestled in my palm.

The Morrigun, but—arrayed as never before.

My breath stopped, and I bit my lip to keep from crying out. I heard footsteps approaching, and I blinked; the pool showed me only my own taut, grieving face now. But the sight of my true self harrowed me only a little less than what I had seen before.

I splashed with my hands, driving the reflection away, then washed my face. Out of the corner of my eye I saw Cernunnos standing beside me. With my face dripping shards of Ladywater, I stood to see what he wanted.

He tilted his antlered head toward the mound of Avalon. "Your mother—now what?"

I looked at her standing at the portal of Caer Avalon as proudly as she had ever stood upon the steps of Tintagel. What, did she think my father was coming home to her? Crazy old woman.

"How should I know?" I grumbled. But clearly we couldn't just send her off. "Wait and—"

But there was no waiting. In that moment, Merlin, no less, stood beside Igraine.

No whirlwind, no flash of light, no commotion. He appeared, that was all, with his staff in his hand and his black dog with the fey white eyes sitting mannerly by his side. Merlin, unchanged in many years, his eyes still like black pits in his bearded face and his druid stone glowing on his forehead.

All those who stood near him gasped and stepped back, but Mother turned to him without fear, smiling. "Well met, sorcerer," she said, her voice queenly.

"Greetings, Igraine the Beautiful." With his starry robe flowing around him, Merlin bowed over her gloved hand. Even in the sunlight, shadows shifted around his head and shoulders.

"You have come to escort me to my son's coronation?"

"Indeed so."

"It was you who sent to me the vision I scried?"

"You guess well, my queen." That sere voice, I had never forgotten it, or the dawn I had first heard it. "Shall we be going?"

I called, "Merlin, wait."

All eyes turned to me as I strode barefoot up the grassy slope to speak with the sorcerer. But I felt Merlin's stare most of all. Still, other than knowing myself to be almost naked compared to my gloved and mantled mother, I did not feel much. I did not shrink, I did not tremble. I had no plan, expected nothing. I wanted to hear what he might say to me, that was all.

He turned his shadowed head toward me, and I looked straight into the blank blackness of his eyes. It was like looking into the endless depth of a starless night sky. "Lady Morgan?" To my surprise, Merlin bowed—but I suppose he was on his best behavior that day. "I beg pardon, Lady Morgan; I did not know you were here! Avalon has sheltered you well."

"I am no lady any longer," I told him.

I suppose there was an edge in my voice, and now I saw black ice in his stare. Still, I faced him levelly. "We have met before," I remarked. "Do you remember?"

"Yes. On the moor, the day of your father's death."

As if it also remembered, the black dog stood up and sniffed my bare knee. I remember the touch of its cold nostrils and the warmth of its breath, although at the time I barely noticed.

Merlin was saying, "You were a child then, and frightened of me." His bearded lips stirred; he smiled like a skull. "But you are not frightened any longer."

I searched inwardly and found no fear. "True."

Merlin asked, "What have you seen in the swan pool, Morgan?"

I smiled, almost laughed. "Horrors—as you know well, is it not so?"

The tautness of his face, like mine. His smile, like mine. "Yes." He looked away. "They tell us to embrace," he said, his voice low, "that darkness we all harbor in our dragonish hearts, they tell us to accept it, befriend it, love it as ourselves. And so they do. To find peace they weaken the beast within, they tame it. But you, Morgan—"

Standing by, my mother interrupted, "Good sorcerer, will you soon be ready to escort me to my son?"

Merlin ignored her, his gaze on me. I grew aware of the circle of fays all around, silent and watching, of Rhiannon standing by my mother's side murmuring something to her to soothe and quiet her.

But most of all I was aware of Merlin, mighty Merlin, standing an arm's reach away from me with the druid stone winking at me like a third eye from his forehead . . . why was I not afraid? Because already I had lived through the worst that could happen to me?

"I, Morgan," I echoed Merlin, mocking, "what do I care for peace, or love either? Look what love has done to me." I thrust my crippled right hand toward him so that he could see the milpreve couched in my palm.

His eyes widened, and his spangled robes rustled as he swayed. I had staggered him.

"They say we choose our fates," I remarked, "but I wonder."

He raised his stare from my hand to my face, and his eyes were not quite blank, black nothings after all; I saw wonder in them. "Morgan," he asked, pointing with his beard toward my palm, "was that done destroying Redburke's army?"

"Yes."

"Then indeed you have reason to question the ways of fate. If it were not for your making away with his most powerful enemy, Arthur would likely not be King today."

His words turned a bitter knife in me, and I think he knew it. I saw the shadow of a smile beneath his beard.

"Would you like to come with us to the coronation?" he asked courteously. "Your sister will be there."

Although I was Arthur's half sister, it had not once occurred to me to be a presence at his king-day. Now I felt a dare and the prodding of a doom I did not understand and a reckless willingness to embrace both. Perhaps I could wreak mischief upon this upstart Arthur? I would enjoy that. "Why not?" I said, very cool, very much the lady indeed. "Yes, thank you for thinking of it. I will go with you."

"You are very welcome." Merlin reached toward my right hand. "May I try my powers upon that?"

All ladylike indifference deserted me. My chest gulped breath and kept it a moment longer than usual. My lips parted but did not speak. I felt some fear now, yet I nodded and lifted my hand toward him.

He clasped it in both of his, and the feel of his hands surprised me, as dry as his voice yet warm and calming. He closed his fearsome eyes, and I saw the shadows gathering thicker around his shoulders—then I closed my eyes as well, for I did not want to see the forms shaping around him. I heard a confused clamor of voices, chitter squeak giggle too dark to be piskies. And I heard fays exclaiming, Merlin chanting, and I felt—power, power almost as fearsome as that of my stone but more controlled, force running up my arm clear to my heart, my shoulder blades, my spine.

Although it did not hurt, I think I screamed, and then there was a weight dropping away from me, and silence in which I felt the black dog licking my knee.

I opened my eyes, my left hand reaching down of its own accord to pat the dog, my right hand hovering before my face whole, healed, as well as the other.

A sunlit gleam of orichalcum drew my glance to the ground. My milpreve lay there in a mass of the silvery metal. As I looked, it fell loose and rolled a few inches into the grass.

I stared at it.

Then I looked up at Merlin. He had stepped back, and it was hard to tell with the shadows settling like a mantle around him, but I thought his face looked gray. Weary.

"Thank you," I whispered to him.

He nodded.

I found my voice. "From my heart I thank you," I said humbly, speaking loud enough for the others to hear as well.

"The day may come when you will not thank me, Morgan," said Merlin in that sere voice of his—it seemed to come out of the wind, from a distance, even though he stood right there. "But yes, we do indeed choose our fates. What will you do with that?" He inclined his head toward the stone lying on the grassy ground.

The milpreve. Already my gaze had gone back to it.

The choice.

"Morgan," came Cernunnos's low voice from my side, "you are far from whole, and peace is a stranger to you. You are further than ever from being ready."

"I will never be ready," I murmured.

"Listen to your heart," he said, and something in his voice made me think with hazy surprise, *He loves me. He knows me truly, the dragon in me, yet loves me.*

He loves all of us.

But love only hurt me.

Gazing at the blue stone, trying not to think, only to know myself, I heard my mother say plaintively, "Good sorcerer, I want to go to Arthur now, please. I want to go to my son."

I knew.

In that moment I knew who I was.

I was the one who would bring down King Arthur.

And if that meant being a smirking sorceress—no, worse, a vulture swooping over the battlefields—then so be it. Damn my fate and damn my future, but only turmoil and black wings and the cackle of a hag made sense to me anymore.

As if my father's spirit whispered in my ear I heard his golden-honey voice: "... *daredevil* ... *firebrand* ... *you are born for trouble, Morgan.*"

I smiled as I bent and picked up the milpreve. It nestled warm between my fingers, bright blue and happy, naked and free. But not for long. From my long loose hair I pulled three strands—I still held the third strand of fate in my never-ready hands, and I meant to keep it. I twisted the strands together into a long fine thread, kissed my milpreve and wished. Yes. I still had powers. I held a strong silk cord now, bright red.

I slipped it through the hole in the stone, then looked around. Rhiannon gazed back at me. Epona. Menwy. Cernunnos.

"I will see you again, I am sure of it," I said, my voice wavering a little, "but I want to tell you now that I thank you and I love you."

I would see them again, but I would no longer be able to speak of love. Fate willing, I would no longer feel love either.

They said nothing. They knew my choice by my need to say those words. Cernunnos stood with his lips pressed tight together, his face pale despite his tawny skin.

I did not look at Merlin, but at somber Cernunnos and sweet Rhiannon, as I reached up and bound the milpreve to my forehead.

Then I looked at Merlin, and he bowed. "I will be honored to escort you to Camelot, Morgan le Fay."

He carried me away on a steed of air, and I did not think to look back.

Epilogue

ONCE AGAIN MISTRESS OF TINTAGEL, IGRAINE STOOD atop the tallest tower, leaning on her cane, her pure white hair piled atop her head and bound with strings of pearls on golden thread. King Arthur had sent a messenger to give her his greeting and tell her he would ride that way, perhaps today. Therefore she stood watching for a first sight of him.

Years ago, Igraine remembered, that messenger might have been Morgan in bird form, a swallow, a swift falcon, or even a golden eagle with a blue jewel shining in the middle of its regal forehead. Igraine shook her ancient head to shake away thoughts of Morgan. Although she had no proof, nothing but a mother's hunch to go on, it still seemed to her that her daughter the sorceress had somehow caused that terrible situation with Arthur and Morgause, the illegitimate child born of incest, Morgause a ruined woman and Arthur—

No. She would not think it. The fate that Merlin had prophesied might not happen for a long time. Might never happen, now that Merlin was gone.

Was that dust she saw rising in the distance, or just her bleary old eyes fooling her? She straightened and peered, but could not be sure. To rest her eyes she scanned her homeland. Rocks against which the sea ever broke and broke its white waves. The fields, the grazing land, the moor, standing stones and quoit stones and furze and—and great antlers, like those of a stag? But no, it was a man, a stranger, riding a white horse—Igraine blinked, and all she saw now were the bare branches of a dead tree. Stupid old eyes. Being a woman was a curse, but growing old was worse. Igraine turned back to watching for Arthur.

Her son, Arthur, High King, blessed ruler, protector of peace—and oh, the fighting it had taken to make him so. And even more lives might have been lost had it not been for Merlin and, yes, Morgan, she and Arthur seemingly friends at first, Morgan wreaking warfare at Arthur's side in the shape of a lion, a dragon, a giant serpent with a blue stone blazing between its mismatched eyes—uncanny. Igraine shook her head again. Utterly uncanny, that girl, and always had been, Igraine had known it from her first look into the midnight of Morgan's baby eyes, one darkest green, one darkest violet. As a young woman, young and foolish and wanting only to be happy, she had looked away from the child and tried to deny it, tried to wish it away. But old now and wiser, she knew better: No amount of wishing would make Morgan go away.

If Arthur had listened to his mother, he would have kept Morgan as a friend, gifting her as he did his other allies with a castle and domain, even though she was a woman.

It was a hard thing to be a woman, and unfair. Even for a queen, it had been—

Igraine forsook all thoughts of the past, leaning heavily on her cane to crane her head forward and look, as if a few inches gained could help her—but yes, surely that was a cloud of dust approaching, and in it the dim forms of horsemen, and a flame-shaped scarlet flag in the fore, and the glint of a golden crown.

Igraine turned and shuffled toward the stairs, hurrying her old feet as much as she could, hunched over her cane. She did not notice the shadow, or the great soot gray bird swooping overhead, the stone glimmering like a blue tear between its uncanny eyes. She did not feel a thing when the dark feather floated down to touch her gently, oh so gently, on the shoulder.